Blac

Black Stockings

Emma Allan

X
LIBRIS

An *X Libris* Book

First published in Great Britain in 1999
by Little, Brown and Company
Reprinted 1999

A CIP catalogue record for this book
is available from the British Library.

ISBN 0 7515 2740 8

Typeset in North Wales by
Derek Doyle & Associates, Mold, Flintshire
Printed and bound in Great Britain by
Clays Ltd, St Ives plc

X Libris
A Division of
Little, Brown and Company (UK)
Brettenham House
Lancaster Place
London WC2E 7EN

Black Stockings

Chapter One

'*SO HOW DO* I look?'

She knew the answer to that. She looked fantastic. She had long, slender legs and the black stockings clung to them like paint. The nylon of the stockings was made from some new process so it appeared so sleek and glossy it looked wet. She had never worn stockings before, only tights, and was astonished how sexy they made her feel. It wasn't only that the jet-black self-supporting welts made the naked flesh above appear, by contrast, impossibly soft and creamy; it was the fact that the tightness of the nylon banding her thighs emphasised that above them she was open and accessible.

'Christ, Letitia, that's unbelievable.'

'I'm glad you think so.'

She was standing in the bedroom doorway of her small flat. It opened directly on to the sitting room. Apart from the black stockings she wore a short black satin slip, its bodice inset with delicate, almost transparent, lace, a present from a long-forgotten boyfriend, which she had never worn before, and her highest black high heels, her long blonde hair brushed out over her shoulders. In fact she had bought the shoes on impulse months ago and had never worn them before, the heels

1

too high to take anything but diminutive steps. They made her legs look even more spectacular, however, stretching and firming the muscles of her calves and thighs and giving her buttocks a distinct pout.

'Do you like stockings?' she said.

She pulled the slip up to reveal the stocking tops.

'I've never seen you wear those before.' His eyes widened as they focused on her thighs.

'They were a present. I went to my interview today at that lingerie company. They gave all the girls a pair. A new material, apparently.'

'Sensational.'

'You know something, Tom, they're having a really odd effect on me.' The sensation of rolling the silky sheer stockings up her long legs had given her a distinct pulse of sexual arousal. She was intensely aware of her body. Her nipples were producing little thrills of sensation as they rubbed against the lace of the slip and her sex was throbbing in a way it usually reserved for more direct stimulation.

'Really?'

'Mmm ... Right here.' She pressed her fingers into her lower belly. 'I think perhaps you should examine me more carefully, don't you? Just in case there's anything seriously wrong.'

She had been going out with Tom Andrews for two months. He was a junior doctor at the local hospital, a nice enough bloke and good company, but in bed she always had the feeling he would rather be doing something else. That was not to say that he hadn't always been conscientious in his efforts to make sure she was satisfied before he took his own pleasure; it was just that she felt, as he toiled away, he would rather have been watching the football.

'Sounds good to me,' he said. Tom jumped up from

the sofa. She was gratified to see a bulge distending the front of his trousers.

She walked back into her bedroom. She had a large double bed, with a brass bedstead. The bed was really too big for the small room, making it impossible to accommodate any other furniture with the exception of a small bedside chest, her clothes and make-up table kept in the second bedroom. She had stripped off the counterpane and draped the bedside light with a red scarf so the light in the room was a rosy glow. She knew exactly what she wanted from him this evening and exactly why.

'Close the door,' she told him as she sat on the edge of the bed.

He did as he was told, then walked over to her. He was just about to sit down beside her when she stopped him.

'No, not yet. There's something I want you to see first.'

She was in a strange mood. She had been like it ever since she'd returned from the job interview this afternoon. Sex was not something that had ever been particularly high on her list of priorities but tonight she needed it. Badly. If Tom hadn't been scheduled to come around to take her out to dinner she would have had to call him and insist he came over.

'See?' Tom said, with a puzzled expression.

Letitia lay on her back on the white sheet, and stretched her body across the bed, her long blonde hair trailing over the pillow. She scissored her legs apart and pressed her hand down between her legs, rubbing the black satin against her sex. The satin felt deliciously cool against her distinctly overheated labia. Gently she wriggled her finger into the folds of her flesh until she found the little nub of her clitoris. It responded with a huge wave of sensation that made her moan.

She had never done anything like this before. She liked sex, she always had, but she had never displayed herself so wantonly in front of any man. She could see Tom's eyes were staring at her, taking in every detail, and that excited her too. She slowly pulled her legs back, bending her knees, the heels of the shoes rucking the sheet up around them.

'Can you see me?' she asked unnecessarily.

'What are you going to do?' he said, his voice strained.

She pulled the black slip up, giving him a clear view of her sex. Her blonde pubic hair was short and stubbly. It had always been that way, never growing longer than a quarter of an inch. Each hair on the triangle of her mons pointed inwards, down towards the apex of her thighs. Between her legs was the same, her labia themselves fringed by the golden blonde fleece but not hidden by it. She began to rub her finger across the top of her clit, very gently, rocking it from side to side. Her other hand moved up to her breasts. She squeezed her right breast under the lace, then pinched at her nipple. It appeared her whole body had been sensitised as this produced another surge of feeling.

She had masturbated before. It was not something she did often, but occasionally, usually as she was about to fall asleep, she would play gently with her clitoris, or squeeze it between her labia by rubbing her thighs together. She knew some women used vibrators or other objects as a substitute phallus but she had never needed penetration to bring herself to a warm but muted orgasm.

But it had never felt like this. Tonight all the feelings were being amplified, every movement of her finger producing a throbbing pleasure out of all proportion to what she normally felt. And she knew why. It wasn't the

4

black stockings. They were a symptom, not the cause. She wasn't performing so outrageously for good old reliable Tom. In her imagination it was not his eyes that were staring at her so intently but those of the man who had sat across the room from her this afternoon during her interview. Matthew Silverstone. Apart from a brief greeting as he'd been introduced, he hadn't said anything to her. He'd sat with his legs crossed and a wry expression playing on his face, as if he understood instinctively how awkward and artificial the interview process was and sympathised with her predicament. Every time she looked his way his eyes, brown eyes the colour of aged brandy, had been rooted to her. Matthew Silverstone was, she decided the moment she set eyes on him, the most attractive man she had ever seen. But it was not only an aesthetic attraction; what he made her feel was a physical need quite unlike anything she'd experienced before.

She felt her clitoris throb wildly. She stroked it faster, and increased the pressure of her finger, pushing it back against her pubic bone. She closed her eyes and got an instant picture of his face, his dark-brown curly hair, his rather square jaw and straight nose, and those brandy eyes that had seemed to look at her and through her at the same time.

'Oh God . . .' she moaned.

Abandoning her breast, she arched her buttocks off the bed and slid her hand under them. With little subtlety she pushed two fingers deep into her vagina, as deep as they would go, until the knuckle of her hand was hard up against her spongy labia. She was astonished at herself. She had hardly ever penetrated herself in this way but she could feel her sex reacting strongly, contracting around the invaders. Her vagina was wet. She could feel her juices running down the slick, silky walls and out on to her thighs. The sensations from her clit increased as her finger moved faster. It seemed to be vibrating, sending ripples of pleasure coursing through her body.

She knew she was coming. All the feelings in her body were coalescing, combining into one. She pushed her body down on to her fingers, trying to get them a fraction of an inch deeper. The inside of her vagina contracted sharply, as the sensations from her clit sharpened, seeming to turn in on themselves, until they were concentrated on this one tiny spot, her whole world focused there. And then the world stood still. It might have only been less than a second, but the gap between being there on the brink of orgasm and tumbling over into it seemed to go on forever, every nerve in her body straining for release. Then she came. Her orgasm exploded, sweeping over her like a wave of heat, making her nerves sing and her body shudder.

Slowly, as the feelings leached away and her muscles relaxed, she withdrew her fingers from her sex. This provoked another prickle of pleasure, like an orgasm in miniature. Her labia quivered.

She opened her eyes. For a moment she had forgotten where she was, her orgasm so overwhelming that it had wiped out everything else. But as it all came rushing back to her she realised that what she felt had only created a hunger for more. It was the hors-d'oeuvres, not the main course.

Tom was standing by the side of the bed, with his trousers and white Y-fronts around his knees, his large circumcised erection sticking out from the tails of his shirt.

'Did you enjoy the show?' she asked.

'You've never done that before,' he said. She had the impression that his tone was ever so slightly disapproving.

'It seems to have had the desired effect,' she said. She scrambled off the bed, dropped to her knees at his feet, took hold of his cock in both hands and fed it into her mouth. Her lips wrapped around the ridge at the bottom of his glans and sucked it hard, then she pulled back and used her tongue, running it all over the smooth pink flesh. She squeezed the base of his shaft hard with one hand while the other slipped between his legs and cupped his balls. He moaned and she felt his phallus throb.

Tom caught her by the shoulders and pulled her to her feet. He held her in front of him for a moment, looking into her eyes as if trying to divine the cause of her behaviour, then pushed her back on the bed, not in the least gently. He grabbed the hem of the satin slip and pulled it up over her hips, then rolled on top of her, his erection pressing into her belly.

The suddenness of all this thrilled Letitia. Sex with Tom was usually a subdued affair, fumbling into position with a politeness and consideration that resembled a tea party rather than the passion associated with the act. But her display, her wantonness, had obviously aroused more than just his cock. He hadn't even paused to strip his trousers and pants from around his ankles.

As she spread her legs open she felt him buck his hips and direct his erection down between her thighs. It was hot and very hard, harder than she ever remembered it being before. She was just about to move her hand down to guide him into her – something she knew he liked her to do – when he simply caught hold of her wrist, pulled her hand away and jammed his cock up into her body, her wetness making the penetration frictionless.

'Oh, that's so good,' she told him, moving her lips up to his ear.

'Mmm . . .' he grunted.

He began moving in and out, not with the slow discursive rhythm he usually used, but hard and very fast, slamming into her as though his life depended on it, his belly slapping against her thighs.

Letitia gasped as his cock filled her. She raised her legs and hooked them over his back, changing the angle of her sex so he slid even deeper into her. She could feel her juices running over him, and hear the squishing noise they made as he thrust up into her.

'Harder,' she said. 'I love it.'

She scored her nails down his back then dug them into his rump to urge him on. He reacted by trying to screw himself even deeper. As he plunged inward, the base of his cock knocked against her clitoris and combined with the sensations in her vagina to set up a pulsing tempo in her body that she knew would inevitably lead to orgasm. Tom's cock was throbbing. Letitia could feel every inch of it. Whether it was her imagination or not she seemed to be able to feel the ridge at the bottom of his glans every time he pulled back. It was catching on an inner contour of her vagina and producing another sharp pang of pleasure to add to all the others.

His pace did not let up. His face was buried in her neck, his whole body rigid, and he ploughed into her with even greater force.

She knew he was going to come. In all the times they had made love they had never come together before, Tom careful to see that Letitia had her pleasure before taking his own. But now she could swear she could actually feel his semen pumping up from his balls and, as his cock went into spasm, her vagina was spasming too.

Suddenly he thrust up into her with every ounce of his strength and stopped, holding his glans at the very top of her sex, while his pubic bone crushed her clitoris. The thick rod of flesh throbbed violently as her vagina closed around it as tightly as any fist. It was as if their two organs were melding together, the feelings in both completely in tune. Letitia felt his spunk boiling up inside him, exactly as all the sensations in her body were doing. As his cock kicked against the tight confines of her vagina, and jets of spunk spattered out, she came too, each spasm producing an exact and equal one in her. They clung to each other, their bodies trembling, both panting for breath.

The moment the feelings subsided, he rolled off her. He lay staring at the ceiling, his trousers still wrinkled around his ankles.

'Oh God, that was wonderful,' she said, almost to herself.

He said nothing. He looked angry.

'What's the matter, Tom?' she asked, sitting up.

'Nothing,' he said. 'Do you want to go out now? I booked a table at eight.' He didn't look at her.

'So we're going to be late. Does it matter?'

'No. I suppose not.'

'You could always ring them and cancel,' she said. Her body was still trembling, every nerve tingling as though it had been given an electric shock. She could feel the thick viscous liquid he had deposited inside her beginning to leak out, and for some reason she found that exciting. She wanted to attack him, to throw him back on the bed and take him in her mouth until she got him hard again. Then repeat the whole experience with her on top this time.

But Tom seemed to have other ideas. He swung himself off the bed and got to his feet, pulling up his underpants. 'I'm hungry,' he said.

And it was pretty obvious he was not hungry for her.

9

'Good morning. Um, I'm Letitia Drew.'

'Oh right, you're the new girl?' The receptionist had black hair that had been dyed a garish blond, the roots showing through the spiky style. She wore a pink blouse and an orange skirt, both in a cheap nylon material.

'Right,' Letitia replied.

'I'm Tracy. If you go through the double doors on the right, along the corridor and down to the end, there's a big red door. Go in there. That's where you'll be working. Andrea's in already. She'll show you the ropes.'

'Thanks.'

'Welcome to BSL,' the girl said, grinning broadly.

'Thanks again.'

Letitia set off down the corridor.

It had been three weeks since her interview with the Black Stockings Lingerie Company. She had been looking for a new job for the last six months. She was working for a clothing wholesale company and was deeply bored. Her role was little more than a shipping clerk, making sure consignments of clothes were delivered to the right destinations worldwide. She had only taken the job in the hope that she would get a chance to move into their design department, but that had been closed down three months ago when the company had decided to concentrate entirely on selling operations.

She had applied for every job vacancy she could find in the rag trade, but unfortunately there always seemed to be a huge number of candidates who had more experience than her, or who, despite her diploma in textile design, were better qualified. So it was to her surprise and delight that BSL had called her the day after her interview and told her she'd got the job, especially as it was a company she really wanted to work for. Working with a major manufacturer on new chemical compounds that could better the elasticity and silkiness of Lycra, the design department had already come up with some startling new designs that were reportedly selling like hot cakes. Letitia was sure the company had a great future. What's more, they had made it plain to her that after an initial two-month probationary period as a general dogsbody in the design department she would be given her own responsibilities, especially in relation to textile design, her speciality. It was exactly the chance she had been looking for.

She opened the red door and walked into a large open studio with a dozen drawing tables and lamps, each with their own pedestal unit containing huge quantities of pens and drawing instruments. Along the walls hung swatches of material and big posters advertising some of the company's past products, panties, bras and corsets, each poster marked in the top right-hand corner with the company logo, a drawing of a pair of glamorous legs sheathed in high heels and black stockings.

Standing on the foot-high rostrum at the far end of the studio was a leggy brunette, her hair cut into a neat bob. She was wearing black silk panties with high-cut legs and a matching bra with a cross-over plunge front, her firm round bosom pushed up by its three-quarter cups. In front of her, sitting on a stool with a sketchpad in her hand, was a redhead in a smart black and white check suit. She appeared to be drawing a picture of the lingerie.

'Andrea?'

'Yes.'

'I'm Letitia. Am I interrupting?'

11

'Hi. Pleased to meet you. Not at all. This is our new range. What do you think? I have to do a sketch for the new catalogue.'

'It's very sexy.'

'Good. That's the idea. Would you like a coffee?' She turned to the model on the rostrum. 'We'll take a break, Madeline. Back in ten minutes.'

'Sure.'

The model picked up a rather dowdy cotton robe and put it on, then went to sit in a battered armchair in one corner of the room, picking up a copy of the *Sun*.

Andrea led Letitia to a little alcove with a sink, a fridge, a kettle and a large coffee machine.

'This is where all the coffee and tea is kept. There's a fridge if you want to bring a salad or sandwich for lunch.' She filled the coffee machine with coffee from a tin, then switched it on. 'This keeps us all going until lunch.'

'So what do I have to do?'

'Joy will tell you that. She's a nice woman. Really. Between you and me, she practically runs this company. She's usually in by now. She was telling me about you. She was very impressed. And so was Matthew, I gather.'

The mention of Matthew Silverstone's name almost made Letitia blush. She had thought a lot about him since she'd heard she'd got the job. She had put the experience with Tom down to an excess of nervous energy after her interview and had determinedly discounted the influence of Matthew Silverstone. If she was going to see him around the office, as she most certainly would, she didn't want to find herself developing some sort of schoolgirl crush, however attractive she found him. But it had been difficult not to indulge herself in more flights of sexual fancy. She had never masturbated more frequently. Alone at night in her big double bed, it had been all too easy to conjure up his face, and those penetrating brown eyes. She'd imagined him telling her what to do, explaining how he wanted her to spread her legs, and let him watch while she stroked her clitoris . . .

'Why do you say that?' she asked, trying to sound as casual as possible.

'He doesn't usually attend the interviews.'

'So why this time?'

Andrea shrugged. 'Don't know. Joy thinks he spotted you in reception when you were waiting to go in and liked what he saw.'

This time Letitia did blush.

'I can't believe that,' she said.

'This is a small company. Rumours run around like wildfire. Take no notice. Are you married?'

'No.'

'Is there a significant other?'

Letitia laughed at that expression. She had never regarded Tom as significant, especially as she'd seen increasingly less of him in the last three weeks.

'No.'

'Well, then it's nobody's business but your own.'

'What do you mean?'

'Just that if Matthew does make a play for you . . .'

'Do you think he will?' Letitia felt her heartbeat increase.

'I have no idea. I told you this place is a rumour factory. But if he does then you can make up your own mind about what you do.'

'Is he married?'

'Yes, though we never see his wife around here.'

Letitia wasn't sure how she felt about that information. She supposed she had better regard it as a relief. She had never been out with a married man and wasn't going to start now, especially not with her boss.

'Andrea!'

A large bulky woman bursting out of a shapeless purple dress exploded through the studio door. Letitia recognised Joy Skinner from her interview. She had done all the talking and Letitia guessed it was Joy who was responsible for giving her the job.

'Hi, Joy,' Andrea said.

'Can you get over to production right away. Have you done that sketch?'

'No.'

'You'll have to leave it till later. Find out what Adam wants. He's panicking about something.'

'Done.' Andrea turned to Letitia. 'See you later,' she said as she rushed out of the door.

'Good morning. Sorry about that. Production is always panicking. Welcome aboard. I see you've found the coffee,' Joy said.

'Yes. Would you like a cup?'

'Yes. But I always get my own. That's one of the rules around here. You're paid much too much to waste time on getting anyone coffee. Remember that.'

'I will,' Letitia said. That, she thought, was a very good start.

'Letitia!'

The voice had startled Letitia. She had been walking back to the studio with a package she'd collected from reception when the double doors had opened and Matthew Silverstone had come up behind her.

It had been exactly a week since Letitia Drew had joined BSL, though she had a strange feeling it had been much longer. Everyone had been so friendly and helpful and the work had been so interesting, it felt like she'd been there for months. Joy Skinner, in particular, was a wonderful boss, motherly, sisterly, professional and non-judgemental all at the same time. She treated Letitia as an equal despite the fact she was clearly not one, in terms of either knowledge or experience.

'Oh, Mr Silverstone.'

'Hello there, how are you? I'm sorry I haven't been here to welcome you personally. Had to fly to New York.'

He was wearing an impeccably tailored grey suit, a white silk shirt, black brogues and a yellow tie. His eyes were looking straight into hers just as they had the day of her interview, and now, as then, she had the feeling he could see all her secrets, her life laid out for him to inspect. Her heart was beating so fast she wondered if he could hear it.

'So how are you settling in?'

'I love it,' she said. There were a hundred things she could have said but she feared she would become tongue-tied. She had forgotten the extraordinary effect he had had on her. She had to remind herself to breathe, and there was a sudden tightness in her chest. She was sure her face was as red as a beetroot.

'Good. Good. Look, when you've finished tonight would you like to come up to my office? I usually offer all my new employees a drink. Bit of a tradition. And as I was away . . .'

'That would be very nice,' she stammered.

'Good. Good.'

Without another word he turned and headed down the corridor. There was a staircase at the end of the passage and she watched as he disappeared out of sight, skipping up the steps two at a time.

She looked at her watch. It was four thirty. She usually left at five. She had half an hour to go.

At ten to five she walked into the ladies' cloakroom

15

and redid her make-up. She wished she had been wearing something more attractive than the plain beige shirt-waister she had put on this morning, then decided it was probably better that way. It was no good entertaining any fantasies about Matthew Silverstone. He wanted to offer her a drink to welcome her to the company. She shouldn't read anything into that, despite what Andrea had told her on her first day.

Letitia knew she was attractive to men. Like a lot of women, she suspected, she had no trouble attracting men in quantity; it was the quality that was the problem. She had a good figure, tall and slender with curves in all the right places, long straight blond hair, and an open face with high cheekbones and a rather small mouth with naturally very red lips. But it was her eyes that she thought of as her best feature, large and bright, with clear whites and deep-blue irises. They stared back at her from the mirror in front of her as she applied a touch of eye shadow, innocent of all intent. Who was she kidding?

At exactly five o'clock she said her goodnights to Joy, Andrea and the other staff in the studio and walked up to the first floor. Matthew Silverstone's office was at the far end of the corridor, a secretary guarding access.

'Hi,' Letitia said to the girl, who she barely knew.

'Hi,' she said. 'I'm Jackie. And you're Letitia, right?'

'Right. Pleased to meet you,' Letitia said.

'Matt's expecting you, go right in.' Her tone was friendly but she wore a grin that suggested she knew something that Letitia didn't.

Letitia walked past the desk and knocked on the large panelled door in front of her.

'Come.'

She opened the door. Matthew Silverstone's office was large. It was on the corner of the building, with windows

16

facing in two directions, though the view across Great Titchfield Street was uninspiring. The office was clean and bright, with white walls and a polished ash floor. There were two steel and black leather chairs in front of a large desk made from stainless steel, a stainless-steel credenza and a long dark-red chesterfield.

Matthew Silverstone sat behind the desk in a high-backed black leather swivel chair. The surface of the desk. apart from a telephone console and a computer monitor, was clear.

'Please come in,' he said. 'Close the door. Sit.' He indicated one of the chairs in front of his desk. 'I was just about to open a bottle of champagne. Does that suit you,or would you care for something else?'

'I love champagne,' she said. She also loved the way his eyes crinkled at the corners when he smiled.

He went to the credenza. A bottle of champagne sat in a modern stainless-steel wine cooler. He opened it expertly, twisting the cork so it did not pop, then poured the wine into two tall flutes. 'Taittinger Rosé,' he said, handing her a glass. 'A real taste of strawberries.'

'Thank you.'

He leant on the edge of his desk and touched his glass against hers. 'Welcome to Black Stockings Lingerie,' he said. 'And apologies for the delay.'

Letitia sipped the champagne. It was delicious.

'How were the stockings, by the way?'

He was looking her straight in the eyes. Did his glance last a fraction of a second too long?

'Sorry?'

'The stockings we gave you at your interview?'

'Oh, right. Sorry, I'd completely forgotten.' But she hadn't forgotten the effect they'd had on her. She felt herself blushing. 'Actually, to tell you the truth, I'd never worn stockings before.'

17

'A lot of women haven't. But they're coming back. We think so anyway. They're so much sexier, don't you think?'

Letitia wasn't sure how to answer that. 'Yes,' she said hesitantly. It was the truth after all. 'And the nylon seemed to be very silky.'

'That's the new process we're developing. Silk used to be the best material for stockings as far as texture and feel were concerned, but it went hopelessly baggy and limp. We're trying to get the same silkiness but with real elasticity. Did you always wear tights?'

'Always. But . . .' She wanted to tell him what an odd effect the stockings had had on her but decided that was too close to the bone. 'If I can find stockings as good as those, I'm certainly going to wear them more frequently.'

'Good.'

He stood up and went to sit behind his desk again. 'Anyway, I hope Joy has made it clear that we encourage what the French call *engagement* at all levels. If you have something to say, if you think we're doing something badly and can do better, if you feel a customer's not being treated right, we want you to say so. No one who works for me has a fragile ego.'

'Joy has made that clear. It's very encouraging.'

'Good. And of course we don't like any sort of demarcation. If you have a design idea then draw it and we'll consider it.'

'I've always been interested in design,' Letitia said. 'I think I mentioned that at my interview.'

'Yes, you did. Well, we'd be interested in seeing what you can do.'

'Really?'

'You see that?' He indicated a small black-framed print of an advertisement on the wall behind his desk. It featured a thin waspie girdle with long suspenders. 'We sold nearly ten thousand. Everyone thought we were mad, that it was too risqué, but the market is changing. Women are going out to buy underwear now to please themselves, but they also want to please their men. And men are buying it too. Do you know, our market research shows that twenty per cent of men go into a lingerie shop or the lingerie department of store and browse. *Browse*. Can you imagine that even ten years ago?'

'No.'

'So we have to cater for that market. And for women who want to be sexy without being tacky. That is really how you'd define our product range, I suppose.'

Other than his first glance, he had given nothing away to suggest he regarded her as anything other than an employee, Letitia thought. He was polite and charming and clearly believed what he said, and if he had any other motivation he certainly did not betray it. The trouble was, she didn't know whether that was a relief or a disappointment. She had never been with a man who had such a marked effect on her. There was nothing about him that didn't fascinate her; the way his mouth moved as he talked, the little habit he had of pulling on his ear, the way he seemed to be completely relaxed and at ease.

They talked for nearly thirty minutes about the underwear market and the rapid changes it was undergoing and finished the champagne. He appeared interested in everything she said and laughed out loud when she told him how her mother had tried to persuade her to wear a pantie girdle when she first went out on dates though her tummy was perfectly flat, convinced that it would act as a sort of chastity belt.

'Well,' Matthew said. 'I mustn't take any more of

your time. I hope we can do this again. And don't forget, my door is always open to new ideas.'

'I think I'm really going to enjoy working here.'

'Where do you live, by the way?'

'Kentish Town.'

'Then can I offer you a lift? I go right by there.'

Letitia didn't know what to say. She supposed she should have refused, but Matthew sounded genuinely solicitous. It was ridiculous of her to assume this was a prelude to anything else. 'Thanks. Anything's better than the Northern Line.'

'Come on then.'

His secretary and the rest of the staff had all gone home and a security guard was manning the reception desk by the front door. They walked out and along the road to a multi-storey car park a hundred yards away. Matthew led her up to a powder-blue Bentley Continental parked on the second floor.

'I've never been in a Bentley,' she said, as he opened the passenger door for her. The car exuded a smell of leather.

'A little ostentatious, I fear,' he said.

He was a good driver, careful and precise. The traffic was heavy and it was hot outside, the early summer sun beating down on the windows, but the air-conditioning kept the car deliciously cool.

'Listen, I don't want you to get the wrong idea about this, but I usually have a swim at my club. We drive right past. As it's been such a hot and sticky day, would you care to join me?'

It had been a hot day, and the thought of diving into a swimming pool was tempting. But alarm bells were ringing. The idea of driving her home might not be as innocent as it had seemed.

'I haven't got a costume,' she said, weakly.

'That's not a problem. They can lend you one.'

'Really?'

She looked at him. Perhaps it was the soporific effect of the big car with its whisper-quiet engine and floating suspension. Perhaps it was the champagne. Or perhaps it was the fact that every time she looked at Matthew Silverstone she felt a knot tightening in the pit of her stomach. Whatever the reason, she suddenly realised that she didn't care about the consequences.

'Then that would be very nice,' she said.

'Good.'

He turned left at the next junction and in five minutes they were pulling into the forecourt of the Caledonian Hotel, a large renovated late-Victorian edifice, where a uniformed commissionaire leapt forward to open the passenger door. Another appeared to drive the car away as they were ushered into the hotel.

'Largest indoor pool in London,' Matthew told her as they headed down into the basement.

The health club of the hotel was luxurious. The receptionist told her that there were several swimsuits to choose from in the changing room, and she found a tight-fitting yellow number that was a little too small for her in the bust but that was cut flatteringly high on the leg.

By the time she had put her hair up and changed, Matthew was already in the pool, doing lengths in an effortless front crawl. She joined him.

'Great, isn't it?'

It was. Her idea of the ultimate luxury had always been a swim at the end of the day. The water was cool and wonderfully refreshing. She was a good swimmer and easily matched Matthew for pace. They swam ten lengths flat out, then changed to breaststroke and did another ten at a more leisurely speed.

'Let's have a Jacuzzi,' he said.

They climbed out of the pool together. Matthew's body was slender and muscular, his chest covered in a mat of hair. His legs and arms were contoured by muscle that was clearly well exercised, his belly flat with not a hint of fat.

'Well, that certainly fits in all the right places,' he said, as he glanced at the swimsuit.

'I'm glad you think so,' she found herself saying, then realised it was true.

The large Jacuzzi was empty. They stepped in together and turned the pumps on, the water bubbling up all around them. Letitia soon found sweat breaking out on her forehead, the water hot and steamy.

'It's great,' she said.

And it was. She looked at Matthew intently. His hair was plastered back against his head and he was sweating too, but this made him even more attractive. She remembered exactly what she had felt the first time she had seen him, the way her response to him had been so physical. If anything, her response to him now was stronger, but she hadn't the faintest idea what she was going to do about it.

'Perhaps this was a mistake,' he said.

'Why?'

'Because I think you're a very beautiful woman, Letitia, and I'm finding it extremely hard to keep my eyes off you.'

'Is that such a bad thing?' she said, trying to remain calm though her pulse was racing.

'Yes, because it means I'm going to make a suggestion you might find unacceptable . . . I don't want to be accused of sexual harassment. That's not my style.'

'I'm glad.'

'So perhaps we'd better go?'

'No,' she said very decisively. 'What is this suggestion?'

He smiled. 'I would like to take you to bed.'

Letitia smiled too. She should have asked him all sorts of questions. What about his wife? Had he done this often? How many other girls from the office had he propositioned? He was a married man and her boss and she knew both were good reasons for not getting involved with him, but she realised she didn't care about any of that now. 'I think I'd like that very much,' she said steadily. Wanting to take the initiative, she slid across the Jacuzzi, put her hands on his shoulders and kissed him lightly on the mouth.

'Your place or mine?' she whispered. She pressed her body against him.

'I can't wait that long,' he said. 'Come on, let's get dressed.'

Chapter Two

UPSTAIRS IN THE foyer he walked over to the reception desk. Letitia watched as he filled in a registration form. She wondered how many other women he had taken in this hotel, but not even that mattered to her. All that mattered was the sexual excitement that was making her whole body tingle. She had never wanted a man more in her life. Night after night over the last four weeks she had thought of him. That had built up the pressure to a point where it desperately needed some release.

They took the lift to the second floor. A large woman in a florid summer dress eyed them suspiciously, their wet hair and slightly bedraggled appearance obviously not meeting with her approval.

The hotel corridor was carpeted in thick green carpet. They walked to the left, following the arrows to Room 243.

'Do you want some more champagne?' he asked her.

'No.'

Letitia felt bold and empowered. She had never done this before. Sex had always come after an appropriate number of dates so she could make a considered judgement as to whether she liked the man enough to go through with it. But she didn't know Matthew

Silverstone at all. And she couldn't honestly say she wanted to. All she wanted to do was tear his clothes off, run her hands over that hard, muscular body and sink herself down on his cock. When life was reduced to such basic elements, it had a great simplicity, she decided.

They reached Room 243.

'Here we are,' he said.

For the second time in an hour, she turned towards him and kissed him, but this time she crushed her lips against his and plunged her tongue into his mouth, pressing her body against him, ironing him back against the wall. She felt his cock stirring against her belly and angled her hips so it was trapped between them. She was behaving like a whore and that excited her.

Matthew broke away. He inserted the key card into the computer lock and opened the door. Then he stooped, hooked an arm under her knees and one around her neck and hoisted her up effortlessly. He carried her into the room, kicking the door closed with his foot.

The room was large and nondescript, a small corridor, with a bathroom on the left and a wardrobe on the right, leading to a rectangular bedroom decorated in toning pinks, the counterpane and the drapes both in the same flowery material.

Matthew carried her over to the low-level double bed and deposited her on it. She kissed him again, and wrapped her arms around his neck, pulling him down on to her.

'I want you so much,' she breathed, her lips moving against his.

His hands started on the buttons at the front of the beige dress. He got as far as the thin belt that banded her waist, then pushed his hand inside and cupped her left breast. Her nipple was already hard. He rubbed his palm against it.

'Let me take my clothes off,' she said.

'No time,' he said.

He kissed her again at the same time as wriggling up to his knees. She felt his hands moving under her skirt until they grasped the top of her tights and her panties and began wrestling them down. She lifted her hips to allow him to strip them down to her thighs. Then he pulled her shoes off and tugged the tights and panties down over her ankles.

Letitia scrambled up and attacked his trousers. She unbuckled his belt and unzipped his fly, then pushed her hand inside to search for his cock. It was not difficult to find. He was wearing white cotton boxer shorts and it was already protruding from their fly. It was large and thick with a lot of very fine blue veins all the way down the shaft. She circled it with her fist, pulled back his foreskin and squeezed it so tightly he moaned. The feeling produced a huge pulse of sensation in her body too.

She sat up and kissed him again, mashing her mouth against his, her excitement spreading through her body like heat. Still holding his erection, as if it were the lever of some strange machine, she used all her power to force him back on to the bed. She couldn't wait to strip his trousers away. Her need was too urgent. Instead, she straddled his hips, settled herself above his cock and guided his glans into the opening of her vagina.

Its heat and its rigidity took her breath away. Immediately she dropped down on it, so it thrust up inside her like a sword, the juices of her body making the penetration instant and effortless. She wriggled her hips from side to side, grinding her clitoris against the base of his cock, her naked thighs rubbing against his trousers.

'Oh God . . .' she whispered, looking down at him.

Something extraordinary was happening inside her. His glans was buried deep in her vagina, so deep she could feel it pressing into the neck of her womb, and from there what seemed to be a wave of liquid was streaming down over him. She had been wet before, but not like this. This was like an ejaculation.

Matthew bucked his hips, pulled out of her slightly, then pushed in again. He reached up and parted her dress, taking hold of the bottom of her white lacy bra and pulling it up so her breasts were exposed. Her breasts were not large but they were round and high with a thick band of aureole surrounding her nipple, its colour only slightly more pink than the rest of the flesh. Her nipples were small and delicate, and, when fully erect as now, were slightly concave at the tip, as though they had been pricked by a pin. He sunk his fingers into them.

Letitia was coming. She could feel her clitoris throbbing as his cock hammered into it. Waves of pleasure were washing over her as Matthew's fingers centred on her nipples, pinching them hard.

'You're making me come,' she said in a voice so clear and crisp it surprised her.

'I can feel it.'

And she knew it was true. Her vagina was convulsing, clutching at the rod of flesh inside it, each new spasm producing another rush of feeling. Matthew thrust up into her once more, then rested back on the bed as she used every ounce of her strength to press herself down on him. Her clitoris, trapped between their bodies, contracted too and she felt a jolt like it had been hit by an electric shock. Some orgasms were long and warm. This was sharp, short and so intense it was almost painful.

But she was not in the mood to rest. As the pangs of pleasure ebbed away she began to tear off the dress. 'What have you done to me?' she asked. She swung her thigh over his hips and felt a huge surge of sensation as his cock was plucked from her sex.

'I could ask you the same question,' he said. He was sweating. She could see beads of perspiration running down his face. It was no wonder. He was still more or less fully dressed, his cock sticking out of the front of his trousers, surrounded by a wet stain. He still had his shoes on.

Matthew sat up. He unbuttoned his shirt, pulled his shoes and socks off then tugged down his trousers and boxer shorts.

'That's better,' he said. He grinned. He had very white, very regular teeth and a neat mouth, his lips as smooth as any women's.

Letitia unclipped her bra and threw it aside, then stooped and kissed Matthew on the mouth. Her lips slid lower, sucking and licking at his neck and his chest. She gathered a nipple between her teeth and nipped it quite hard, noticing the fact that this made his cock jerk. She applied the same treatment to the other nipple with the same result, then began working her way down over his belly. She grabbed his cock in her hand and gobbled it into her mouth greedily. She wanted this now. She sucked on him hard, tasting her own juices, then forced it into the depths of her mouth, so deep she had to control the reflex to gag.

'Mmm . . .' he moaned.

She could see that his dark pubic hair and his balls were soaking wet. Reaching down between his legs, she took his balls in her hand and squeezed them gently as she pulled him out of her mouth. This time she used her lips to suck along one side of the hard, veined shaft, right down to the base then back up again.

'That's enough,' he said. 'You'll make me come.'

'Don't you want to?'

'Not like that.'

'How then?'

'Like this.'

He knelt on the bed, then crawled around so he was kneeling behind her, his cock nudging into the cleft of her buttocks. He took hold of her hips and pulled her back against him.

Letitia fell forward, supporting herself on all fours. The proximity of his sex to her vagina immediately made it throb again. She opened her knees and felt his cock slide down between her labia. It nestled into the mouth of her vagina. It felt incredibly hot.

Matthew's right hand moved over her hip and down her belly. As his glans nosed into her vagina she felt his finger delve into her labia to find her clit. The moment he felt the little nut of nerves he pressed it back against her body. At the same time he used all his considerable strength to thrust his erection into her, producing a double surge of sensation that made her gasp.

'You're so wet,' he said between clenched teeth. 'So wet and so tight. I love it.'

Letitia was too wired to reply. It was as if her first orgasm hadn't gone away, just laid low waiting for the chance to reassert itself. His cock and his finger had immediately revived all the delicious feelings she had experienced before, every nerve in her body singing the same soaring song.

He started to move. As his finger moved on her clit, pushing it from side to side, he began to pump into her sex, pulling almost all the way out, then lunging powerfully back in again, the silky walls of Letitia's vagina so wet she could hear them squishing sibilantly.

The sensations that were coursing through her body were so powerful they were almost overwhelming. In seconds she was on the brink of orgasm again, each thrust taking her closer to the precipice. Her whole vagina was throbbing rhythmically and it was the same tempo he was using on her clit, each tiny movement of his finger producing a huge rush of feeling. The two sources of pleasure began to coalesce, the rapture complete. She shoved her buttocks back on him, felt her sex locking around his cock and came, every muscle in her body rigid, every sinew stretched. She threw her head back and let out a long, low moan that seemed to quiver at the same pitch as her body, her breasts, hanging down vertically from her chest, trembling violently.

His finger slipped from her clitoris but he did not stop pumping into her. He took her hips in both hands and pulled her back on to him as he lunged forward, thrusting his big, hard erection deeper inside. She knew he was going to come. She could feel his cock spasming. He was increasing his speed, pounding into her faster and faster, his belly slapping against her buttocks. His power, his eagerness, was totally exhilarating. She knew she would be able to feel his ejaculation deep inside her and, what was more, despite the two orgasms she had already experienced, that it would make her come. She had never felt so totally open, so completely prone to sensation.

Matthew slammed into her one final time, his hands on her hips holding her so tight she could not move. He pulled his cock back ever so slightly and came. She felt his cock bucking against the tight confines of her vagina, then hot spurts of liquid spattered up into her, one after another. Immediately her body reacted. Her sex contracted fiercely, clamping around the hard rod of flesh and creating a massive reaction, her nerve endings, already tenderised by so much sensation, set alight. Her clitoris pulsed prodigiously and she lurched into an orgasm so intense it dwarfed the two that had gone before, the pleasure raw and undiluted.

It was a long time before either of them moved, so long in fact that it was the sensation of Matthew's cock softening and slipping out of her body that finally roused her.

'God,' she said, rolling on to her side. 'That was incredible.'

'I know,' he said. He lay on his side too and kissed her lightly on the lips.

She might have thought she would feel awkward and gauche now the passion had subsided, but surprisingly she felt comfortable with him. She nestled her head against his arm.

'Do you want something to drink?' he asked.

'Don't you have to get home?'

'Yes.'

'You're married, aren't you, Matthew?'

He laughed. 'I suppose the girls told you that. Actually we're getting a divorce. We don't get on. I don't think we ever did.'

'It doesn't matter. I knew what I was doing.'

'It's true,' he said.

'I'd have slept with you even if you'd been blissfully happy, Matthew. You just had this effect on me. Ever since I first saw you. Some sort of chemistry, isn't it? Pheromones? Isn't that the latest theory? I'd never been susceptible to it before.' She looked at his cock. It was flaccid now, wrinkled and wet, the glans retracted back into the foreskin. She ran her hand down his body and stroked it lightly with the tip of her finger.

'I'd like to do this again,' he said quietly.

'So would I. Very much.'

'If you keep doing that, we'll be doing it again sooner than you think.'

'Really?'

She slid down the bed and slipped his cock into her mouth. To her amazement it began to grow again almost immediately.

'You're right,' she said, sitting up and grinning. 'Do you want me to stop?'

'No.'

And she didn't.

Letitia was sore, deliciously sore. Her nipples ached and her clitoris seemed to tingle when she walked, rubbing against the silky material of her panties. She felt as if she were floating, the edges of her body blurred, her contact with the real world not at all solid. It was a wonderful feeling.

Matthew had told her he had to go to Paris for two days but would be back on Wednesday, when he hoped they could have dinner. She, in turn, hoped 'dinner' was a euphemism for sex.

If she were being sensible, of course, she would have told him she wasn't available and that it had all been a terrible mistake. She was asking to get hurt, she knew that. However much she tried to tell herself she could divorce sex from emotion, she would inevitably become involved with him and he would, equally inevitably, decide to stay with his wife.

But perhaps becoming involved wasn't an inevit-ability. She didn't think she had ever felt this way about a man. She knew nothing about him, other than

32

the fact that he was the managing director of the company for which she worked, and that he was married. What was more, she didn't want to know anything else. It was irrelevant. The only information she needed was when he was going to see her again and take her to bed.

All her life Letitia had believed in the connection between relationships and sex. At college she had had a couple of one-night stands, hot, anonymous gropings that had not been without a crude satisfaction. After that she had told herself that sex was a function of emotion and restricted herself to lovers whom she knew and respected and with whom she was emotionally involved. But what had happened with Matthew had broken all the rules.

She had decided that last night was the best sex she had ever had in her life. The fact that it was with a man whom she had known for barely an hour made her wonder if the lack of emotional involvement was part of the reason why she had responded so unequivocally. With all her previous sexual liaisons there had always been complications, questions of what the other partner liked or wanted or expected, or what they would think of her. With Matthew none of that mattered. There was only one *raison d'être*: sex.

She was sure Tom had gone off her so rapidly because she had shown him a side of herself that did not fit in with his expectations. She still was not entirely sure what had happened that night. Matthew had caused her outrageous behaviour, she knew that, as though somehow he had communicated a sexual agenda to her. Looking back now, the way she had behaved with Tom, wild and open and totally uninhibited, was exactly what she had been like last night with Matthew himself. But whereas Matthew had encouraged her and obviously enjoyed her passion, Tom had, she was sure, felt it more than a little bit disgusting. Before she had always played a role with him, rather coy and undemanding, allowing him to make the running, because that was what she'd felt he wanted. And to be honest, she wasn't at all sure that wasn't what she wanted too. But as soon as she'd abandoned that role, though he may have been too turned on not to play her game, he clearly had not liked it, and had obviously decided she was not the woman he'd thought she was.

Sex had never been her forte. She had always enjoyed it but had always felt something was missing. Up until now she had blamed herself, imagining she had a low sex drive. Now it appeared it was just a question of finding the right stimulus.

She was glad that the studio was busy. Two days were going to pass slowly and she needed work to distract her. But the new catalogue was going to press in a month's time and there was an endless stream of designs to be perfected, produced, then photographed in preparation.

At lunchtime Joy asked her to take some papers up to Matthew's office to await his return. Even the mention of his name caused Letitia's pulse to race.

Jackie was eating a sandwich at her desk.

'Joy wants him to see these,' Letitia said, handing over the file.

'Thanks. I'll see he gets them. How did you get on last night, by the way?' Jackie was a petite brunette, with a round, doll-like face, a tiny nose and small dark-brown eyes. She wore a tight white blouse and a mini-skirt that showed off rather chubby legs. Her face was entirely covered with a pancake make-up that gave her a light tan.

'Last night?' Letitia said innocently.

'You came up here for your welcoming libation, remember?'

'Oh, right. It was very nice, thank you.'

'Have you got a minute?' Jackie said, putting down the sandwich.

'Not really.'

'Just sit here for a second, will you?'

Letitia hesitated, then sat down on the straight-backed chair at the side of the desk.

'Do you mind if I give you a bit of advice?'

'As long as I don't have to take it.'

'Matthew's a charming man. Very attractive. Very sexy. He's also a complete arsehole, if you'll excuse my French.'

'I don't see . . .'

'Let me guess. He offered you a lift home, right? It's on his way. Then he suggested a swim at his health club? Then it's up to a bedroom in the hotel. Am I right?'

Letitia felt her face flush. 'I don't see that is . . .'

'Any of my business. No, you're right, it's not. But women are all supposed to be sisters, right, so I'm just warning you. It's a standard routine, Letitia. Anyone who comes to work here who's even halfway pretty – and let's face it, you're gorgeous – gets the treatment. I know what goes on. I see the bills from the hotel.'

'So what's the advice?'

'Just don't get too involved. Look, there's two kinds of lines that married men use – you knew he was married, didn't you?'

'Yes.'

'Well, they either tell you they're happily married but their wives are not really into sex. Or they say their marriage was a terrible mistake and they're getting a divorce. Matthew uses the latter, am I right?'

Letitia nodded.

35

'He's not getting a divorce. He's been married for fifteen years. His wife is quite something. She's in the rag trade too. I just wanted to mark your card, that's all.'

Letitia got to her feet. She wasn't at all sure what her reaction to all this was. She thought of telling Jackie that she had gone to bed for one reason and one reason alone, that she wanted him so inordinately it wouldn't have mattered who or what he was. Instead she merely said, 'Thanks.'

'I think he's a bastard,' Jackie added.

'Why do you work for him then?'

'He's a charming bastard. Men are children, aren't they? If you give them a toy they'll play with it until it's broken. Matthew hasn't broken his yet.'

'And you? Has he taken you swimming?'

Jackie nodded. 'On my first day. But that's as far as it went. I often wondered what it would have been like.'

Letitia avoided the temptation to tell her. 'I'd better get back.'

'Matthew's back tomorrow.'

'I know,' Letitia said with an enigmatic smile.

'I'll pick you up at eight.'

'Where are we going?'

'Does it matter?'

'I'm aching.'

'Where?'

'You know where.'

'If I think about that I'll get an erection.'

'Think about it then.'

'See you at eight.'

Letitia put the phone down. He had an extraordinary effect on her. The sound of his voice made her nipples stiffen and her sex pulse. No man had ever done that. She had been in the shower when the phone rang and

36

she'd run out into the sitting room naked, dripping water on the stripped-pine floor. He'd got back from Paris at six, he'd told her, and wanted to see her as soon as possible.

She put the phone down and walked back into the bathroom, using a towel to mop up the trail of water she'd left on the floor. She dried herself too, then walked back into the bedroom.

She hadn't really thought about what Jackie had told her. A year ago, perhaps as little as a month ago, her reaction would have been very different. There would have been a great deal of wailing and gnashing of teeth. But Matthew Silverstone had changed all that. She knew precisely what she wanted from him and she knew how to get it. She wasn't looking for commitment. All she wanted was sex.

She had laid out her clothes on the bed. Last time, in the Caledonian Hotel, she had been wearing a white bra greyed by too many washes, and white cotton pants. This time she intended to look altogether more alluring. One of the advantages of working at BSL was that there were plenty of samples lying around in a great variety of shapes and sizes and styles. She could take her pick.

After what Matthew had said in his office, stockings, black stockings naturally, were her first choice. After the effect they had had on her the first time she had tried them on, stockings were a sort of symbol of her new attitude. The tights she had always worn before formed a barrier against sudden, impulsive sex. They were protective and isolating. Stockings, on the other hand, did not have to be removed. They left her feeling totally unrestricted.

Joy Skinner was working on a black basque made from satin, with a tightly cinched waist, long black suspenders and a low-cut wired bra made from almost transparent lace. There were thong-cut black satin panties to match. They had looked sensational on Madeline as she'd stood on the rostrum in the studio. The bra pushed her breasts together into a deep cleavage, and the suspenders snaking over her hips made her long legs look even longer. The panties revealed the creases of her pelvis and clung tightly to the triangle of her mons. As the model was more or less Letitia's size, she was sure it would fit.

She pulled on the basque and fastened the series of hooks into the eyes at the back, using the tightest of three possible positions. As she worked her way up from the bottom to the top and the feeling of constriction increased, she felt her excitement growing with it. She settled her breasts comfortably into the bra cups, then looked at herself in the mirror on the back of the bedroom door. She had never worn lingerie like this. Hers had always been a sensible approach, and most of the underwear she owned, with the exception of one or two gifts from boyfriends perhaps giving her a heavy hint, was cotton. She had never thought of lingerie as an adjunct to sex. But she had to admit the black satin and lace not only made her look sexy, it made her feel sexy too.

In fact, now she understood the effect it could have, she had already started to work on her own designs. That was one practical benefit of her new-found sexual freedom.

Sitting on the bed, Letitia unwrapped a packet of stockings. They were made from the same experimental material as the pair she had been given at her interview, and were silky and soft to the touch. She rolled one into a pocket then inserted her toe, amazed at the way the glossy material seemed to transform her flesh, encasing it in a sheen of shadowy black. She rolled the second stocking on in the same fashion, then clipped the front and side of the stockings into the long suspenders that hung down from the hem of the basque. The suspenders pulled the jet-black welts into peaks on her thighs.

She stood up and examined herself in the mirror again. The short blond hair on her mons seemed to be framed by the basque at the top, the long black suspenders at the sides and the stocking tops at the bottom. Once again the welts of the stockings had made her thighs look soft and incredibly creamy.

The black panties lay on the bed. She picked them up and stepped into them, drawing them up her legs and over her hips. Her clitoris reacted strongly as the silky material nestled against her sex. Letitia didn't think she had ever been so aware of it. She ran her hand down over the gusset of the panties to try and soothe it but this only made matters worse and it throbbed energetically as her fingers stroked against her labia.

In the mirror she watched as her hand glided down between her legs, caressing the black satin. She looked like a whore, an expensive whore admittedly, but one dressed to do business. The thought excited her.

She sat back on the bed and glanced at the alarm clock on the bedside table. It was six forty-five. She had plenty of time. She lay back, allowing her head to sink into the feather pillow, and closed her eyes. The lingerie definitely made her feel different. The fact that the basque and the stockings clung to her so tightly made the area at the top of her thighs feel, by contrast, free and unprotected. Still with her eyes closed, she ran her hand down along her side. It went in sharply at her waist then out over her generous hips. The feeling of the slippery satin was arousing.

She allowed her hand to run all the way down to the

tops of her stockings, the tactile differences between her flesh and the material quite marked. Then she brought her hand up again and angled it inward, her fingers burrowing under the leg of the panties as she eased her legs apart. She touched the top of her labia and immediately felt a buzz of sensation. She was thinking about Matthew. She could see those dark eyes looking at her, calmly, dispassionately, and most of all knowingly. He knew what she was like. He knew what she could offer him.

Suddenly she dug her fingers right down into her labia, then thrust them into her vagina. She was wet. She knew she would be. She was sure she had been wet from the moment she'd drawn the stockings up her legs. Her sex spasmed as she twisted her fingers around, trying to screw them deeper into her body, remembering how Matthew's cock had invaded it so completely, knowing that it would be there again tonight.

She had no intention of masturbating, she told herself. She rolled her head to one side and stared at her body in the mirror. The long suspenders stretched across her thighs like fingers, so tight they cut into her flesh. She saw her other hand move down under the panties, distending the taut black satin as her finger arched inward to find her clit.

'No,' she said aloud.

But it was too late, much too late. Her body was alive, crawling with luscious sensations. She wriggled her shoulders from side to side so her nipples would rub against the comparatively coarse texture of the bra. They responded with a tingling of pleasure that was routed straight down to her sex. In the past she had never needed penetration. Now she needed it like nothing else. She slipped another finger into her sex,

40

making three in all, the mouth of her vagina stretched by their breadth. She tapped at her clitoris hard, then ironed it back against her pubic bone and held it there, the soaring pleasure spreading out rapidly. She was coming.

In the mirror she watched her body arc up off the bed. She saw the surprise and delight that was shining in her eyes. But she saw nothing else, her eyes forced closed as the wave of orgasm reached the nerve endings behind her eyeballs. Her head was pushed back so far the sinews of her throat were corded like rope. She said one word, loudly and very clearly.

'Matthew.'

'Where are we going?'

'You'll see.'

He'd taken her to dinner at a small French restaurant in Soho where the staff had all addressed him by name and the food had been exceptional. Then he'd walked her up Poland Street towards their offices. But instead of going in through the plate-glass doors at the front of the building, he'd led her round to a small alleyway at the back. He used a key to open a dingy wooden door and ushered her through into a little passageway littered with the empty cardboard bolts from the material they used and boxes of 'cabbage' from the cutting room floor. At the end of the passage was the metal door of a small lift. Matthew pressed the call button and the door slid open. The cabin was just big enough for two.

'BSL is owned by Green Gross Friar Holdings. They converted the top floor of the building into an executive apartment,' Matthew explained. 'I use it whenever I have an early flight or an early meeting in town.'

'And naturally you have a very early meeting tomorrow?' Letitia said.

'Naturally.'

'You mean I get all night with you?'

'All night. Except I'll have to drive you home in the morning to change. You can't come to work in that outfit. I hear the managing director is very puritanical.'

Letitia was wearing a ruby-red sleeveless silk sheath dress with a turtle neck and a teardrop cut-out that revealed a lot of the cleavage the tight basque created. The skirt was long enough to cover the tops of her stockings, but only just.

'Oh, he is,' she agreed, pressing her back into him and wriggling her hips from side to side so the silk whispered against his suit.

The lift rose to the top floor. It opened on to a small but immaculately decorated corridor, completely different from the mess downstairs. Matthew took out his keys again and opened a large lime-wood door inlaid with an art nouveau design of zigzags in a much darker wood.

Inside, the apartment had been designed like a New York loft, a large living space with the metal pillars that supported the ceiling all exposed and the walls stripped back to the original red brick. There was an ultra-modern kitchen area with stainless-steel units and granite work surfaces in one corner, and a huge oval dining table made from a sheet of inch-thick plate glass in the middle of the room, surrounded by twelve dining chairs, after the style of Charles Rennie Mackintosh. Opposite the kitchen were two long, wide oatmeal-coloured sofas facing each other in front of a black matt-finished steel-flared chimney, below which was the grate for a log fire.

'Quite a place,' Letitia said. 'Where's the bedroom?' She was in no mood to be shown the finer points of the interior designer's art.

'Over here.'

Matthew led the way across the room to another inlaid lime door. He opened it to reveal a minimalist interior. There was a double bed covered with a grey tweed counterpane, a single bedside chest with four drawers made from highly polished rosewood, and a wall of flush-fitting wardrobes, the doors running from floor to ceiling, their plain surfaces painted a matt grey. The atmosphere was unmistakably masculine.

'And the bathroom?' she asked.

He went to the wall of what Letitia had thought was all wardrobes and opened the grey door at the far end. She saw that it led to a large bathroom tiled in a light-grey marble. The bathroom suite was black and there was a large circular bathtub sunk into the floor.

'Very impressive,' she said. She kissed him lightly on the cheek. 'Give me two minutes.'

'Do you want another drink?'

She shook her head.

In the bathroom she stared at herself in the long mirror over the bath. She quickly brushed her fingers through her hair, then unzipped the red dress and stepped out of it. She smoothed the basque over her body and adjusted a slight wrinkle in one of the sheer stockings, tightening the suspenders.

They had talked business over dinner. Matthew was good at his job, she thought. He knew the market and she was sure he was absolutely right in pushing the lingerie business from the practical to the glamorous. It was what women wanted. She was a case in point. There was a time when she would have eschewed the overtly feminine basque and black stockings, taking the view that it was not up to her to ensnare a man with such fripperies. But what she had not understood was the effect they had on her. They asserted a sexual

43

agenda. It was extraordinary how quickly her attitude had changed. Perhaps in the past she had been more interested in finding a man with whom she could make a commitment and sex was no more than an after-thought. But that was before she'd discovered that sex could be something completely wild and wonderful. For the time being, at least, she wasn't interested in a long-term relationship. What she was interested in was sexual gratification.

She opened the bathroom door and strode into the bedroom. Matthew had stripped off the counterpane and was lying on the bed. He had taken off his suit and was wearing a white cotton robe.

'Is that one of ours?' he asked, his eyes roaming her body. 'My God, Letitia, you look gorgeous.'

'I'm glad you approve.'

He scrambled up on to his knees, caught her by the hand and pulled her towards him, stretching up to kiss her on the mouth, his arms wrapped around her back, his hands caressing the tight black satin of the basque. As his tongue pushed between her lips she met it with her own, the two dancing together, hot and wet.

He began to pull her down beside him. In a graceful choreography, their bodies still entwined, they lay on the bed, Matthew's large erection now pressing into Letitia's belly. He caught the waistband of her panties in his hand and began to pull them down. She arched her buttocks off the bed and allowed him to tug them away.

He began to kiss her neck, then ran his mouth up to her left ear, using the tip of his tongue to circle the inner whorls, his hot breath making her moan. But as his mouth moved down to the top of her breasts she stopped him.

'No,' she said. 'Not yet.'

'What then?' he said, looking puzzled.

'I want to show you something first.'

'Show me?'

'Take your robe off.'

He unknotted the white belt of the cotton robe and pulled it off. His erection sprung up from his loins, his glans trying to force its way out of his foreskin.

'Lie back,' she said. She was dressed like a whore and now she intended to behave like one. She had planned exactly what she was going to do.

Matthew lay back on the cream sheet. Letitia got to her knees. She swung her thigh over his chest so she straddled his body, facing his feet, then inched herself back until her sex was poised above his mouth. He took this to be an invitation, grabbed her by the hips and levered himself up so he could plant a kiss on her labia.

'No, you've got to wait,' she said sharply.

'Wait for what?'

'Just do as you're told.'

He did. He lay back and stared up at her, every detail of her sex, from the fourchette of her labia at the base of her mons to the little puckered crater-like depression of her anus, neatly framed by black lingerie. It was as though she could feel his eyes roaming her body, producing an invisible ray that made her tingle. She knew her sex was wet and was sure he would be able to see it. She squirmed her knees a little wider apart and felt her vagina wink open; the movement created a jolt of sensation.

Letitia slid her right hand down over the smooth satin of the basque and on to the short soft hairs that covered her mons. She had varnished her nails in a much deeper shade of red than she usually used and knew he would be able to see the brightly painted fingernail of her middle finger parting her labia. Though she had braced herself against the shock of sensation as her finger touched her clit, it still took her breath away. Her body was already responding at fever pitch, and she knew it was because she had never behaved like this in her life.

She saw his cock jerk up from his belly reflexively as she rolled her finger from side to side. Slowly, trying to control her reactions, she snaked her left hand down over her buttocks and into her sex from the other side. With two fingers she probed the mouth of her vagina, then pushed them in, thrusting them up until her knuckle was hard against her labia. She began to pump them in and out. How many times in the last weeks had she done this, using both her hands to bring herself off while she imagined Matthew Silverstone watching her? Now he was here, so close she could feel his breath on her thighs, able to see everything she was doing in minute detail.

She felt her labia pulse. Her clitoris was alive. She could feel it throbbing under her finger, moving of its own accord. Inside her vagina too her flesh was rippling as her fingers thrust forward. She looked down at her body, her breasts pushed out by the tight bra, the black stocking tops pulled into dark chevrons on her thighs, her hand buried between them. The tightness of the basque was adding to her excitement, she knew. She had never looked like this, or felt like this.

In seconds she was ready to come. It was not just the physical sensations that were driving her on but the mental ones too. She felt a peculiar sense of power. This was her agenda, exactly what she wanted to do, and that was another cause of arousal. Before, in bed, she had always allowed herself to be led by the man. Now she had found a way to express herself and had taken charge in a way she had only done once before, briefly, with Tom. That event had had the same inspiration.

Matthew Silverstone had turned her sexuality upside down.

She thrust her fingers into her vagina one more time. In her mind's eye she could see Matthew staring up at her, his face framed between her thighs. On the tiny nut of her clitoris she found an even tinier place, the most sensitive spot on her body, and flattened her finger against it, causing a rush of sensation that triggered all her other nerves. Suddenly she was engulfed in a spiral of pleasure, her senses rocked. She straightened her back and cried out loud, only just managing to hold her fingers in place.

But before the feelings had leached away she felt Matthew's hand on her left wrist. He seized it and pulled her fingers out of her vagina so abruptly it made her shudder. He wrapped both hands around her thighs and pulled her down towards him until her sex was planted squarely on his mouth. She felt him kissing her labia, squirming her lips against them and plunging his tongue into her vagina.

Instead of fading away, Letitia's orgasm was instantly renewed. Another huge surge of pleasure, as sharp and potent as the first, erupted from her loins. Reflexively she pushed down on his face and felt his nose burying itself in her soft flesh.

Letitia tried to regain some semblance of control. Men had done this to her before but it had never felt like this. Her body was shuddering and her mind was seemingly overwhelmed, so many new sensations assailing it she simply couldn't keep track of where the next wave of pleasure was coming from. She loved what his lips were doing to her labia, sucking at them and drawing them into his mouth, each little tug causing a massive surge of delight.

His tongue bulldozed her finger aside on her clitoris

and lapped at it forcefully, jamming against the little promontory and pushing it upward. Then he began to wind his tongue around it, circling it with the regularity of the second hand of a clock.

The reactions were so sharp she thought she had come again but it was difficult to be precise because what she was feeling now was so extreme, so unlike anything she had felt before, she could not categorise it. It was like being set adrift in a sea of sensation with no rudder or sail to steer by, wandering helplessly as the waves tossed her about. She had not planned this. She had planned to tease and tantalise him, not be overcome by his first assault.

She made a determined effort to fight her way out of the miasma. She opened her eyes and grabbed his erection with both hands, as fiercely as a drowning man grabs a line. It was her line to pull herself back under control. But it didn't last long. As she pulled back his foreskin and leant forward to gobble his cock into her mouth, it was almost as if she had pushed it into her vagina. There seemed to be a direct connection between the two, both hot and wet and ultra-sensitive. As she felt Matthew's erection spasm in her mouth, her vagina spasmed too, just as strongly as it would have done if he had been buried in that.

She tried to hold on, but once again a wave of passion threatened to engulf her. She felt Matthew's hand caressing her buttocks, then suddenly his fingers were thrusting into her, two at first and then a third, stretching her labia so tautly they tingled. It was extraordinary how different it was to be penetrated by someone else's fingers rather than her own. She felt her sex squeezing around them as if to test their strength, and oddly this caused his cock to twitch too. He pushed them deeper then twisted them around, suddenly coming into contact with some inner nerve that recoiled with a pleasure as acute as anything else she'd felt. She fought desperately to control her feelings, trying to concentrate on him, squeezing his cock with one hand while she pumped up and down on it with her mouth. But it was a losing battle. What she was doing to him was affecting her quite as much. The feelings generated by his hard, throbbing erection in her mouth and his long bony fingers probing the pulpy flesh of her vagina were sending messages to each other, the double penetration a great deal more thrilling that the sum of its parts. Letitia sucked hard on his cock, jamming it deep into her throat, felt her vagina contracting around his fingers with an equal force, and came, a burst of pure pleasure that racked through every nerve she possessed.

'Well, I must say, that was quite a show.'

For a good couple of seconds Letitia was too caught up in the wonderful sensations that were playing through her to register the voice. But, like waking from a deep sleep to the sound of an alarm, something somewhere finally got through and she opened her eyes and sat up in fright, Matthew's cock popping out of her mouth with a plop.

'Good evening.'

Standing in the bedroom doorway was a slender but curvaceous woman wearing a white St Laurent suit with cream satin braid around its lapels and hems, sheer cream nylons and white Gucci shoes with a spiky heel. Her hair was auburn in colour, thick and glossy, styled in soft waves that fell on her shoulders. She had a gold bracelet on her left wrist and a Cartier wedding ring on her third finger, together with a massive emerald set in silver. It was difficult to guess her age, because her skin was flawless and seemed to radiate a youthful energy, but Letitia guessed she was in her late thirties. Her face was rather long and pinched but her bright-green eyes and fleshy mouth gave her a sensuous quality that was far from unattractive.

'What the hell are you doing here?' Matthew said, scrambling out from under Letitia's body.

'Don't worry, dear,' she said to Letitia. 'I'm his wife. She's really something, Matt. I admire your taste. Does she give good head?'

'Let's talk about it out there, shall we?' he said, nodding towards the bedroom door. 'This is nothing to do with her. It's between you and me.'

'That's your opinion.' The woman began to unbutton her jacket, advancing across the room. 'Did he tell you we were getting a divorce? That's his usual line.'

Matthew grabbed the white cotton robe and put it round Letitia's shoulders.

'How chivalrous.' The woman wasn't wearing a blouse under the jacket, only a white lace bra. Her breasts were large and billowed out of the low-cut cups, displaying a healthy tan.

'What are you doing, Ursula?'

'Isn't it obvious?'

'I think I should be going,' Letitia said, looking around for her panties. Unfortunately they were right at Ursula Silverstone's feet.

'Is this what you're looking for?' Ursula said. She dipped her knees and scooped the panties up. 'You won't be needing these for quite a while.' She tossed them to one side.

'I'm going to go,' Letitia said.

'Let her go, Ursula. This is between you and me.'

'So you said.' She reached behind her back and unzipped her skirt. Wriggling her hips, she allowed it to drop to the floor, then stepped out of it. She was wearing a broad white lace suspender belt and matching bikini-style white panties. The suspenders were clipped into stockings, the opaque white welts making her tanned thighs, by contrast, look even browner.

Letitia stood up. She went towards the bathroom, where the rest of her clothes were.

'What a good idea. Run us a bath, would you, sweetheart? A nice warm bath.'

'Look, Mrs Silverstone, I just think I should go,' Letitia said.

'Ursula, I can explain.'

'So can I. So can this very attractive blonde. We can all explain. The point is that I warned you what would happen if I caught you again, didn't I?'

Matthew said nothing.

'Didn't I?' Ursula repeated.

'This was all a mistake,' Matthew said, his voice thin and reedy.

'No, Matthew, it was not a mistake. Letitia Drew here is not a mistake. You went to her flat and picked her up in your Bentley, then took her to dinner at Chez Vallon. She works for Joy Skinner, I understand.'

'How did you find that out?'

'Does it matter?' She reached behind her back and unclipped her bra. She had big, pendulous breasts that slanted up slightly at the ends like a ski slope so that her rather small nipples were actually pointing upwards. 'For Ms Drew's benefit I suppose I ought to explain. My husband here has been philandering for the last couple of years. I'm not a jealous woman by nature, but I am a woman who enjoys sex. It has got to the point where Matt seems to prefer other women to me. And I'm not prepared to accept that. So I told him that if he did it again there would be a price to pay. As you're an employee of BSL it's a price you're going to have to pay too.' She sat on the edge of the bed and unclipped one of the white suspenders from its stocking. 'Now go and run a nice deep bath for me. You go too, Matthew, and explain the situation to her.'

'Come on,' Matthew said, taking Letitia's arm. He led her into the bathroom and closed the door.

'What is all this?' Letitia said, her mind spinning.

'She's serious.' Matthew turned on the bath taps.

'About what?'

'We've got to do what she says.'

'You've got to do what she says. I'm going home,' Letitia said.

'The parent company of BSL is owned by Piers Green.'

'*The* Piers Green?'

'Yes.'

'The moral rearmament Piers Green?'

'Exactly. Ursula threatened to go to him if I ever . . .'

'Piers Green owns a lingerie company. That doesn't seem very likely. From what I've heard, he thinks women should stay at home cooking and raising children.'

'I know. But if Ursula tells him about us, we'll both be out of a job.'

'I don't see why.'

'He's made a lot of fuss about family values and adultery. He fired four people last year for having affairs.'

'Oh Christ, I don't want to lose my job. It took me ages to get anything decent and I really like it.'

'So we've got to do what she says.'

'What do you mean?'

'Play along with her, humour her.'

'She's taking her clothes off out there.'

'Please, Letitia. She's not playing games. I know her. If you want to keep your job . . .'

She gave him a dirty look, which would have finished him on the spot if looks could kill, but didn't know what else she could do. She certainly didn't want to spend another six months trying to find another job. And even if she got one she doubted it would offer the opportunities BSL promised.

'Now isn't this cosy?' Ursula Silverstone walked into the bathroom and closed the door. She was naked apart from a pair of high-heeled white satin slippers that must have been kept in one of the wardrobes. She had a narrow waist and a flat belly, and Letitia guessed, from the contours of her arms and legs, that she spent a lot of time in the gym. Her auburn pubic hair was thick but had been carefully trimmed into a neat triangle. Her tan was not marred by any marks from a bikini; she obviously sunbathed in the nude.

Letitia found herself staring. She'd seen naked girls at school in the showers but that was a long time ago. Ursula was no girl. She was a mature woman, with an exceptionally attractive body.

'What do you want me to do?' Letitia said, quietly, unable to work out what her real feelings were any more.

'Nothing you haven't done before,' Ursula said in a much sharper tone. She nodded at Matthew's now completely flaccid cock. 'He's no good to me in that condition, is he now? Why don't you get him nice and hard? It looked like you'd made a pretty good job of it before.'

'Don't be ridiculous, I'm not doing that in front of you,' Letitia said.

'And I thought you'd have explained it all to her by now,' Ursula chided.

'I did,' Matthew replied.

'So?'

Matthew looked at Letitia and she stared back at him. She could see the three of them in the long mirror above the bath, her black lingerie in stark contrast to their naked bodies.

Inwardly Letitia shrugged. She had no choice. It was as simple as that. Ursula was clearly set on humiliating them both and had lucked into an extremely effective way of doing it.

Letitia dropped to her knees on the cold marble floor. She picked Matthew's cock up with one hand, pulled back his foreskin and fed it into her mouth.

'That's better. Does that feel good, Matt?'

'Why don't you just let her go. It's not her fault.'

Ursula kicked off the slippers and climbed into the big sunken bath. She turned off the taps, poured some heavily scented bath oil into the water, then knelt in the tub with her arms over the side, facing her husband.

Letitia was sucking so hard her cheeks were dimpled. She was astonished that despite the situation Matthew had already begun to swell rapidly.

'Is he nice and hard?'

'Yes,' Letitia said, pulling her head back to reveal Matthew's erection. She still had her hand wrapped around its base and found herself displaying it for his wife, twisting it this way and that.

'Good. Now bend over the wash basin and let me see what he can do with it.'

'What!' Matthew protested. 'Have you gone mad?'

'No, Matt. I'm just having fun. Now do it.'

Letitia got to her feet. Her feelings were totally confused. She felt mortified at being caught with Matthew, and embarrassed by the position she found herself in now, but to her astonishment she also felt aroused. Greatly aroused. Ever since Ursula had walked into the bathroom she had felt little trills of feeling emanating from her sex. And she knew exactly why. When she was at college she had shared a flat with another girl, whose attitude to sex had been completely different from hers. Whereas Letitia was always careful and circumspect about who she slept with, spending weeks getting to know them before she took the plunge, Mandy, her flatmate, would drop her knickers at the first sight of a man, seemingly any man. She was also in the habit of having sex all over the flat, in the kitchen, the bathroom and the hall. One night, a night Letitia had never forgotten, she had found Mandy bent over the kitchen table, her jeans and cotton panties pulled to her knees, while a large front-row forward from the rugby club took her from behind. Neither of them had appeared perturbed at Letitia's presence and had continued as if nothing had happened. In fact, Mandy had asked her if she wanted a turn with him.

The experience had left its mark. Letitia could still remember the expression in the man's eyes, and the sight of his cock, thrusting in and out of Mandy's sex and glistening with her juices. She'd rushed to her room but had always wondered what it would have been like to stay, to accept Mandy's offer, to take her place bent over the kitchen table, while Mandy watched. It was an incident she had wondered about for years, a memory that had rapidly become a secret fantasy. It was the idea of being watched that excited her most, though she had never worked out why, of having someone else in the room while she was *in flagrante*. If she was not in the right mood, or was faced with a particularly unin-spiring lover, she had used it, quite deliberately, to arouse herself, imagining a pair of eyes focused on her.

Not that she had ever attempted to make her fantasy

come true. She hadn't taken sex that seriously after all. Until now. Now Ursula's suggestion had revived all those undercurrents of excitement she had felt that night, and she had her own needs too. Glancing at Matthew, she took two steps towards the wash basin.

'What are you doing?' he said. 'We're not going to perform for her.'

'I thought you said we had no choice?' Letitia said.

'She's a sensible girl, Matt.'

Letitia lent over the black basin, opening her legs and pushing her buttocks into the air. She was intensely aware of the fact that her labia were open and exposed, her short pubic hair hiding nothing. In the mirror above the basin she could see Matthew Silverstone and his wife both looking at her, and that created a pulse of arousal deep inside her vagina. Matthew's anger with his wife had not diminished his erection, his foreskin still fully retracted.

'What are you waiting for, Matt?'

Reluctantly Matthew came up behind Letitia. He put his hands on her hips and directed his cock down between her buttocks. Immediately Letitia's body tensed. The smooth glans slipped down to the entrance of her vagina, then nosed inside. She felt as though her labia were pursing to kiss it. Then he thrust it inside her, and starting pumping into her with all his considerable strength, pulling her back by her hips as he lunged forward.

Letitia gasped. It was the first time he'd penetrated her tonight and his cock filled her completely, as hard and as hot as it had been before. She had been looking forward to this moment for two days, but she had never dreamt it would be under these circumstances. Her sex was alive, every nerve on edge. She wriggled her hips from side to side and looked up into the mirror, her eyes bright with excitement. She could see Ursula leaning over the edge of the bath, watching intently.

Each thrust hammered into the solid core of arousal that Letitia felt deep in her sex, provoking it to produce sharp pangs of pure pleasure. However shaming and embarrassing, she knew she was going to come; she simply couldn't stop herself.

'Oh God . . .' She closed her eyes and threw her head back, her long blond hair sweeping across her shoulder blades. She felt Matthew's hand slipping over her hip and down between her legs. But almost at the exact moment it butted into her labia and found her clit, her orgasm roared through her body. Matthew thrust into her and held himself there, her sex spasming around him. In her mind's eye all she could see was Ursula's gaze boring into her.

'Well, now I see why you were so keen,' Ursula said. 'She's a hot little bitch, isn't she? Now it's my turn. Come over here, Matt.'

Matthew pulled himself out of Letitia's sex. He walked over to the bath, then got in, kneeling behind his wife and immediately thrusting his gleaming erection down between her legs.

'No,' Ursula said. 'I want her to do it.'

'Do what?' Letitia said.

'Get in here with us.'

Letitia began to undo the clips of her suspenders, the aftermath of such a powerful orgasm leaving her ener- vated.

'There's no time for that,' Ursula said. 'Just get into the water.' Ursula's tone was absolutely imperious, brooking no dissent. There was no doubt she intended to be the ringmaster of this particular circus.

Despite her exhaustion, Letitia felt little twinges of

sensation tweaking at her clit. She kicked off her shoes and climbed into the bath. As she knelt in the warm water it washed over her sex, giving her another shock of pleasure. The water immediately soaked into the stockings and black satin, dragging them down. It was an odd sensation. In other circumstances it might have been unpleasant but there was nothing tonight that was not turning her on.

'Get hold of him,' Ursula said, her voice suddenly more throaty. She tipped her buttocks up in the air, half out of the water. Her labia, pursed between them, looked as if they had been shaved, the deckled flesh completely hairless. 'Guide him into me, Letitia.'

Letitia did as she was told. She was so excited again that she was trembling. She took a firm grip on Matthew's erection and pushed it down between Ursula's buttocks as he inched forward. She saw it nestle between her rather thin labia.

Matthew thrust forward.

'Yes. Now fuck me, you bastard. Give it to me.'

Matthew did just that, hammering into her as hard and as fast as he had into Letitia, the water slapping against the sides of the bath. It slapped against Letitia too, wallowing against her sex and creating new waves of feeling. She jammed her hand down between her legs and flattened her palm against her labia in a hopeless bid to stop her clitoris pulsing. In fact it had the reverse effect and created a new dynamic, her battered labia responding with a sharp pang of pleasure that took her breath away.

Ursula had heard the tiny gasp this caused and had turned her head to look at her.

'You love it, don't you?' she said.

'Yes,' Letitia breathed, because it was true. She had never been so turned on.

'Then kiss me.'

And without a moment's thought, Letitia did exactly that.

Chapter Three

'IS THAT LETITIA DREW?'

'Yes.'

'Oh good. It's Ursula here.'

Letitia had been sitting at her desk in the studio when the phone rang. She felt her hand beginning to tremble and her face flush at the mention of Ursula's name.

'Yes.'

'So cold. You're weren't so cold last night.'

'What do you want?'

'Are you busy on Saturday night?' She laughed. 'Perhaps I should put that another way, considering the circumstances. If you have plans for Saturday night you'd better cancel them. I want you to have dinner with me.'

'Dinner?'

'Yes.'

'I don't think that's a good idea.'

'Letitia, I'm afraid I don't care what you think.'

'Why me?'

'You'll see. Have you got a pencil? I'll give you the address.' She dictated an address in Highgate. 'Eight sharp. Don't be late.'

'And if I say no?'

'If you want to keep your job – and Matthew's, come to that – you'd better be there, Letitia. Good afternoon.'

The dialling tone erupted on the line.

Letitia put the phone down. Joy Skinner, in black leggings and a big shapeless green sweater that hid her amorphous curves, was looking at her.

'Problems?' she asked.

'No, just a personal thing.' She went back to collating the colour options on all the items that would appear in the catalogue, co-ordinating what materials would be used for what items, with what colours they would be available in. But she found it hard to concentrate.

The telephone call had come completely out of the blue. She had assumed, when she had climbed out of the bath, stripped off the sodden black lingerie and got a taxi home in the red sheath dress with only the black panties for underwear, that she would never hear from Ursula Silverstone again. She imagined Matthew would not want any further contact either.

She couldn't say she hadn't known what she was getting herself into; Jackie had seen to that. She had broken her own golden rule and got caught doing it, and she felt thoroughly ashamed of herself. She never wanted to see Matthew Silverstone again. She was going to keep her head down and get on with a job she was enjoying more and more each day. That was the main thing now.

She felt ashamed of her sexual feelings too, the fact that she had responded so unequivocally to such a perverse scenario. But that was not all she felt. The intensity of her excitement was difficult to forget. Ursula had tapped into a current in her sexuality that had remained hidden and secret for years but which was unbelievably potent. She shuddered as she thought about what they had done.

There was another element too, which was a great deal more problematic. She had experienced one of the strongest responses of the night as Ursula had looped her hand around her neck and pulled their mouths together. It was the first time she had kissed a woman and she could remember exactly how it had felt, the softness and angles of her mouth completely different from a man's. Instinctively she had cupped one of Ursula's large breasts, digging her fingers into the pliant flesh, and that too had provoked a sharp reaction in her sex, an almost overwhelming urge to do more. It was an urge she had resisted. She had never been aware of any lesbian impulses before and was certain she did not want to cultivate them in the future. She had convinced herself during the course of the day that the reason she had felt such a strong reaction was the fact that her whole body was so turned on, that she would have responded to anything or anyone. It was a case of overstimulation, of sexual overload.

As soon as Joy had left for the day, Letitia put her work aside and climbed the stairs to the first floor. It seemed strange that her night of almost purple passion had happened in this building, right above her head.

'Is he in?' she asked, as she walked along the corridor to Matthew's office.

Jackie was sitting at her desk, typing on her computer keyboard. She gave Letitia a knowing look. 'Sure, help yourself.'

Letitia knocked on Matthew's door, then opened it without waiting for an invitation.

'Hi,' he said. He was on the dark-red chesterfield with photographs of models in BSL lingerie spread all around him.

'We've got to talk.'

'What's the matter?'

'After last night you ask me what's the matter?'

'I got the impression you enjoyed yourself.'

'It wasn't what I'd have chosen.'

'Me neither. However . . .' He cleared the photographs and gestured for her to sit.

Letitia sank down beside him. 'I've just had a phone call from your wife.'

'Oh, I see. What did she want?' His expression changed.

'She wants me to go to dinner at your house on Saturday.'

'What! But I'm away. I'm going to Milan tomorrow for five days.'

That news made Letitia turn cold. She'd imagined that what Ursula wanted was a repeat performance of last night. But if Matthew was not going to be there, it looked as if she had an entirely different scene in mind.

'You mean she's planning to finish what she started last night? What am I going to do?'

'You have to go,' Matthew said earnestly.

'I don't have to do anything, Matthew.'

'You know what she's threatened. She'd do it too. Piers has always liked her. He wouldn't wait to hear my side of the story. I'd be out and she'd make sure you went with me.'

Letitia sat gloomily with her head in her hands.

'I'm not into all that.'

'You were last night.'

'That was in the heat of the moment. And nothing much happened. I couldn't . . . I mean, I wouldn't want to . . .'

'She's not going to ask you to do anything like that.'

'Is she into women?'

Matthew hesitated.

'Well, is she?'

63

'Yes. We have a very open marriage. She likes to have her girlfriends and doesn't mind if I play around.'

'As long as you don't neglect her. Isn't that what she said last night? And presumably that's exactly what you've been doing.'

'I suppose I thought she was content with the way things were.'

'So why ask me to dinner when you're not going to be there?'

Matthew shrugged. 'Look, she probably got the wrong end of the stick. I was there, remember? I saw you kiss her. You were quite enthusiastic. She probably thinks you're bisexual too. You've only got to explain to her that it was your first time and it's really not your scene. It *was* your first time, wasn't it?'

Letitia nodded.

'Well then . . . She's not going to rape you. She's not that bad.'

'I don't want to go.'

'You've got to go. You really have. I'll make it up to you, Letitia, I promise.'

He tried to put his arm around her but she shrugged him off. 'I think we're in enough trouble, don't you?'

Saturday came around slowly. She had been over her alternatives a hundred times. She had even dreamt about Ursula, though the dream was indistinct and she could only remember her waiting dressed in a bright-yellow dress at the front door of a large house. When she'd got inside, the house had been completely empty and Ursula had insisted on showing her every room. She'd started awake after the first four or five.

She had no choice. She had to go. That was what she had decided. The job at BSL was too good to lose. She had read about Piers Green and was certain that

64

Ursula's threat was no idle one. He liked his employees to be squeaky-clean. Any hint of impropriety and they were out. He said men who were having affairs spent more time thinking about their mistresses than they did on their work. He was probably right.

She liked Joy Skinner, and the work was interesting. What was more, Joy had told her they were specifically looking for a new teddy to add to their range. When Letitia had shown her the sketch of the idea she'd been working on, Joy had liked it and promised to show it to Daniel Travis, the head of design. If he approved, it would go into production. Letitia would be able to fulfil her ambition to become a designer. She would never find another opportunity like that.

It was a case of closing her eyes and thinking of her future.

She supposed, if she were honest with herself, that part of the reason for her decision was curiosity. Since Matthew Silverstone had walked into her interview five weeks ago, something had changed in her. She guessed he had just been in the right place at the right time. It was not him in particular that had wrought such a fundamental change, but the fact that he had embodied a desire that she had been unable to express up until that point. Unconsciously her sexual psyche was looking for something it had lacked, a new freedom, and had used Matthew Silverstone as a means to an end.

What had happened on Wednesday was just an extension of that. Her sexuality, woken from its slumber at long last, had not frozen at the prospect of such a bizarre experience, but had relished it. And there was no doubt in her mind that relish was the right word. She remembered exactly how she had felt as Matthew had pounded into her while she was bent over the wash basin. The peculiar fantasy she had cherished for so long had at last become a reality and she had barely been able to contain her excitement. Considering that minutes earlier she had been shocked and totally abashed, was clear evidence, in her book, that her body was asserting its own agenda.

The same was true of the kiss with Ursula. She had felt no revulsion. If the truth were known, what she had felt was desire. At first that idea had shocked her. She had come to an accommodation with herself that what she had felt was just a case of overexcitement. But over the last two days she had faced up to the fact that it might not have been only that. She could remember in detail what Ursula had looked like as she walked into the bathroom wearing nothing but the high-heeled white satin slippers; her big upturned breasts and flat stomach and her thick pubic hair. She had begun to wonder what it would be like to kiss her again, and to press her own naked body into Ursula's. It looked like she was soon going to get the opportunity to find out.

At seven thirty she ordered a taxi. She would charge it to BSL and get Matthew Silverstone to sign her expenses claim personally. She had chosen her clothes with care. For all her devil-may-care attitude about what might happen, she certainly wasn't going to wear stockings, or BSL lingerie. She opted for a comparatively new matching white cotton bra and panties, already turned grey by too many washes, a pair of buff-coloured tights, and a simple black cocktail dress with a modest box neck and a knee-length skirt. She certainly didn't want to give any hint of what she expected. It was, after all, possible that Ursula wanted to do no more than talk about her errant husband.

The traffic on Saturday night was heavy and it took

nearly thirty minutes for the taxi to wend its way up to Highgate, where it pulled through a wooden gate into a circular carriage drive in front of an impressive Queen Anne house.

With her pulse beginning to race, and a fluttering feeling in the pit of her stomach, Letitia rang the door bell.

'Good evening, Ms Drew, how nice to see you.'

Ursula had answered the door herself. She was wearing a tight bright-blue silk bustier embroidered with white flowers that clung to her narrow waist and crushed her big breasts into a dark cleavage, making them balloon up towards her chin. Under this was a long, figure-hugging black silk skirt that was split to mid-thigh, her legs sheathed in very sheer champagne-coloured nylon. She wore black suede high heels with a gold motif on the toe. As before, her hair was brushed out in soft waves down to her shoulders.

'Come in, please,' she said, with no warmth.

Letitia walked inside, feeling distinctly plain in comparison to the older woman.

The house was impressive. The walls were covered in a dark-green silk and the elaborate panelled doors and architrave had been stripped back to the original wood. There were several oil paintings on the wall and Letitia recognised at least two Seikerts.

Ursula opened the door to the right and led the way into a vast sitting room, equally tastefully decorated. Much to Letitia's surprise, standing by the large Adam fireplace, its grate filled with a huge display of dried pink and white roses, were two men.

'Andrew Beveridge, Stewart Copley, this is Letitia Drew.'

'Good evening, Ms Drew,' Andrew Beveridge said. 'This is a pleasure.' He looked at Letitia with undisguised interest, his eyes lingering at her bosom. He took her hand and kissed her fingers. 'Very nice,' he said to Ursula.

Andrew was a short man with a receding hairline and a round, chubby face. Though he wasn't fat, he had an incipient bulge developing around his waist. Stewart Copley, on the other hand, was an attractive man. He was tall and slender, with a full head of dark-brown hair. He had a rather craggy face with a square chin, and large blue eyes that had an unmistakable invitation written in them, unmistakable as far as Letitia was concerned, at least. They were come-to-bed eyes.

'Good evening,' Letitia said, shaking his hand.

'Nice to meet you,' Stewart Copley said. He was equally blatant in his examination of her body.

'And you,' she said, feeling distinctly uneasy.

'Well, isn't this cosy?' Ursula said, looking suggestively at Letitia as she did so.

Letitia remembered the last time Ursula had used those words, and felt a dull pang of desire.

'We're drinking champagne. Is that all right for you?'

'Yes, thank you.'

There was a maid in a black dress and white apron standing at the back of the room, and Ursula nodded to her. The girl immediately picked up a champagne bottle from a silver cooler on a side table and poured the wine into a straight-sided flute. She brought it over to Letitia.

'Cheers.'

There was a clinking of glasses and a sipping of wine, under cover of which Letitia tried to work out what was going on. This was definitely not what she'd expected.

'She's gorgeous,' Andrew told Ursula.

'Absolutely,' Stewart agreed.

Letitia thought that was odd. She was standing right in front of them, so if they wanted to compliment her they could have done it directly.

'I'm glad you think so,' Ursula said. 'Andrew and Stewart run Girl Talk.'

'Really?' Letitia had thought their names were familiar. She had read about them in the trade press. Girl Talk was the fastest-growing chain of boutiques in Britain, with over three hundred stores.

'Ursula is trying to persuade us to buy her new line,' Stewart said.

'And she can be very persuasive.'

'Let's go into dinner, shall we?' Ursula said. She took Andrew's arm and walked him across the sitting room into a wood-panelled dining room. It overlooked a stone-flagged patio that bordered a large rectangular swimming pool. Beyond was a vast lawn, and several huge horse chestnut trees.

The meal was delicious, a cold soup followed by rack of lamb with red-wine sauce. There was a selection of French cheeses, a chocolate soufflé and a silver-tiered stand of *petits fours* to go with the demitasse cups of strong espresso coffee.

The conversation was mostly about business. Ursula discussed the various options on her product range, while Stewart made notes in a palmtop computer. It was only as the coffee was served and the maid took orders for liqueurs that Andrew turned his attention from Ursula to Letitia.

'This must be very boring for you,' he said.

'Not at all. I'm in the rag trade too.'

'Really?' Andrew looked astonished. 'How come?'

'I work for Ursula's husband.'

'Hear that, Stewart, Letitia here works for Ursula's husband.'

Stewart started to laugh. 'My God, Ursula, you are liberal-minded.'

'Not at all. I hear she's very talented,' Ursula said, with a broad grin, obviously sharing the joke.

'I want to go into lingerie design,' Letitia said, not understanding what was going on.

'Well, that's sensible, I suppose. I mean, you must get to know exactly what a man likes,' Andrew said.

'I bet,' Stewart added.

'Shall we go through into the sitting room?' Ursula suggested.

As the two men walked ahead, Letitia grabbed Ursula's arm and stopped her in her tracks. 'What was that all about?'

'What was what about?'

'That stuff about my job?'

'Oh, I'm sorry about that. I suppose I should have warned you.'

'Warned me about what?'

'They're under the impression that you're, how shall I put it, a whore.'

'What! Why should they think that?'

'Because I told them you'd go to bed with them after dinner, both of them. Oh, don't worry, apparently Andrew only likes to watch.'

'What!'

'Don't look so surprised. You behaved like a whore with my husband. It shouldn't be difficult for you. And it will do my business a great deal of good.'

'I'm not sleeping with them.'

'Fine. If that's your decision. You know the consequences.'

'What about you?'

'What about me?'

'Why don't you go to bed with them?'

70

'I hope you're not suggesting I should be unfaithful to my husband?'

Letitia was so astonished she was standing with her mouth open. She stared at Ursula, her hand still holding her arm and her heart beating so hard she could hear it in her ears.

Ursula smiled, a neat, thin smile. 'In fact, I suggest you go upstairs and get ready. I wasn't sure whether you always dressed like a twenty-pound hooker or whether that was just for Matthew's benefit, so I left some stockings out for you. BSL stockings, naturally. Men like that. First door on the left at the top of the stairs.'

'I . . . I'm not. . .' Letitia hadn't the faintest idea what to say.

'You'd better make your mind up,' Ursula said, unsympathetically. 'What did you think? That I asked you here for a cosy dinner and a little chat?'

'I thought you asked me here to go to bed with *you*.'

Ursula laughed. 'Now there's an idea.'

'Does Matthew know about this?'

Ursula's smile broadened. 'Of course. I discussed it with him.'

'You discussed it with him? When?'

'Yesterday.'

'And he agreed?'

'It wasn't for him to agree or disagree, was it? That's up to you. Matthew is in the same boat as you are, my dear. You were both playing with fire. And you both got burnt. I don't believe in getting angry, Letitia, just in getting even.'

Letitia was literally speechless. She couldn't think of anything to say.

'And don't tell me it was Matthew's irresistible charms. You knew he was married.' It was perfectly true, she had known.

An explosion of laughter erupted from the sitting room. The two men were standing holding large brandy balloons, their faces wreathed in smiles. Stewart turned and caught Letitia's eye, winking at her in a way that she could now only interpret as suggestive.

'I think the natives are getting restless. So what are you going to do? Do you know how many people Joy Skinner interviewed for your job? Fifty-five. Everyone wants to work for BSL.'

Ursula turned on her high heels and strode back into the sitting room, leaving Letitia still standing in the dining room.

She could understand why Matthew hadn't phoned her to warn her. He was obviously desperate to keep his job, and was afraid that if he had told her what Ursula had in mind she wouldn't turn up. But Letitia had convinced herself that she was prepared to go to bed with Ursula to save her job. Stewart Copley was an attractive man. If she had met him in the street she might well have ended up sleeping with him after an appropriate interval of time. She had short-cut that interval with Matthew. To save her career, was she prepared to do the same thing with Stewart?

Of course there was another element. Andrew wanted to watch, wasn't that what Ursula had said? Letitia's reaction to that idea at least was unambiguous. Her old fantasy reaching back across the years looked like coming to life again. Its resonance gave her an almost sickly feeling of excitement, exactly in the way Ursula's sudden intrusion had done on Wednesday night.

She had to make a decision. It was now or never. She took a deep breath.

'Well, gentlemen,' she said, marching up to Stewart, 'What does a girl have to do to get a drink around here?'

'What would you like, my dear?' he said.

Letitia wrapped her hand around his upper arm and swayed her body against him. 'Brandy.'

The maid had gone back into the kitchen, so Ursula crossed to the big black-laquered cabinet at the back of the room where all the booze was stored and poured Vieux Hine for Letitia and herself. She handed Letitia a glass, then clinked hers against it. 'Cheers,' she said pointedly.

'Cheers,' Letitia said, turning to look at Stewart. 'Here's to adventure.'

'Adventure?' he queried. She saw his eyes slip from her face down to her body, openly ogling her breasts.

'You're feeling adventurous, aren't you? I certainly am.' She had decided that if she was being cast as a whore she had better behave like one. She squeezed his arm. She could feel the hard muscles of his biceps. 'Nice,' she said. 'I bet you work out.'

'Three times a week, actually,' he said.

'Mmm . . . I like a strong man.' She swigged back her brandy. 'Well, if you'll excuse me, I'm going to lie down.' She put the glass down on an occasional table and walked out of the room, swinging her hips from side to side, only too aware of the three pairs of eyes that were following her.

As she mounted the stairs she felt her heart beating as strongly as it had before. Her show of bravado had done nothing to quell her trepidation, but oddly it had created a growing sense of arousal. The way Stewart had looked at her, the way his eyes had roamed her body with no pretence of anything but pure sexual interest, was arousing. In his eyes she was a whore hired for the evening to entertain him. The idea of being thought of in that way, far from enraging her as she might have expected, was surprisingly freeing. It

73

relieved her of the need to be herself, to react how she would normally react. She didn't have to show any interest in Stewart as a person. All she was there to do was to have sex with him.

Her relationship with Matthew had been so instant that it had almost been reduced to its constituent parts, and she guessed that was one of the reasons it had been so exciting. There was a forbidden element, for her at least, in having sex with a man she hardly knew which gave it extra spice. Years of conditioning and inhibition had been abandoned. Well, tonight was the ultimate test of that hypothesis. And if it did excite her, if her theory proved correct, Andrew's presence, watching everything they did, would only add fuel to the fire.

Or would it? Was she just kidding herself? Would she find her new-found sexuality vanished the moment Andrew walked through the bedroom door? Her fantasy had seen her through one such encounter. But there was no guarantee, however deep-rooted, that it would necessarily excite her again.

She opened the first door on the left at the top of the stairs. It was a large bedroom decorated in shades of blue, with a thick dark-blue carpet, light, flowery drapes that matched the counterpane on the king-sized double bed, and plain dark-blue walls. There was a white-tiled en suite bathroom to the right and a large French walnut wardrobe with an elaborate entablature.

Lying on the bed was a scarlet velvet heavily boned waspie not more than a foot wide, and a pair of BSL's sheer, glossy black stockings. Ursula clearly regarded a bra and panties as surplus to requirements.

Letitia closed the bedroom door and walked over to the bed. As she looked at the lingerie she felt a strong pang of exhilaration.

She could still turn around and walk out, she told

herself. But if she were honest with herself she did not want to go home. She wanted to save her job, but that wasn't the only reason she did not head out of the door and hail a taxi. This was just as dangerous as what she had done with Matthew, if not more so, but it was the danger she was beginning to savour.

Quickly she went into the bathroom. She stripped off her dress, then peeled off her tights and panties. Back in the bedroom she sat on the edge of the bed and picked up one of the black stockings. She rolled it into a pocket around the toe then began playing it out over her leg. The clinging, silky material felt cool against her flesh. She pulled the second one on then picked up the waspie. It was so tight she had to breath in while she fastened it around her waist, but the constriction created a thick pulse of arousal. So did the sight of herself in the mirror that hung on the bedroom wall when she stood up to clip the stockings into the long suspenders that hung down from the corset. She undid the cotton bra and threw it aside. Her breasts quivered. She climbed back into her black high heels and looked in the mirror again, shaking her shoulders from side to side to make her breasts shake. Now not only was she playing the whore, she looked the part.

'Are you ready for me?'

The door had opened a crack and she could see Stewart's hand grasping the edge.

'No. Wait.' She got the tone just right, she thought. She didn't have to bother with pleasantries. Stewart Copley wasn't knocking on her door because he liked her personality; there was only one thing he wanted from her.

She stripped off the counterpane. The bed was made with a light duvet and a pale-blue sheet. She peeled back the duvet and lay on the sheet in the middle of the bed, just as she had done that night with Tom, bending her knees and opening her legs, the heels of the shoes creasing the sheet. She covered her sex with her hand, pressing her palm into her labia. She was not surprised to find that they were already wet.

'All right,' she shouted. She rubbed her hand up and down between her legs. Stewart opened the door. He had taken off his jacket and tie and unbuttoned his collar. His eyes lit up as he saw what she was doing.

'I like to see that,' he said.

'Do you?' she replied with what she hoped sounded like sublime indifference. She wondered why Andrew had not followed him into the room. Perhaps he'd had a change of heart.

Stewart walked over to the bed and stared down at her. 'I don't usually do this sort of thing,' he said diffidently.

'Are you going to get undressed?' she said, ignoring that remark.

He unbuttoned his shirt and pulled it off. He had a deep hairless chest and a flat abdomen. His arms were heavily muscled. He sat on the bed and pulled off his handmade shoes and his silk socks, then stood up and unzipped his trousers. He was wearing black silk briefs.

'Do you want to watch me?' Letitia said. The anger she had felt at what Ursula had asked her to do, and any apprehension, had been overwhelmed by her sexual urges. The excitement she had felt as she walked upstairs had solidified, a hard knot of desire focused on her clitoris. She allowed her finger to venture down into her labia as if to confirm it. She moaned as it found the object of her quest.

'Is it sensitive?' he asked. He slipped his briefs off. His circumcised penis was semi-tumescent, its smooth pink glans slightly larger in diameter than the shaft that supported it. He sat at the foot of the bed and managed to drag his eyes up from her body to her face.

'Yes.' She rolled her fingers over the little nut of nerves. Her body felt as if it had been wired up to some source of sexual energy that was amplifying all its responses. The tiniest of movements was creating huge waves of sensation.

His eyes had gone back to her sex. She could see his excitement and that in turn excited her. He was a stranger, a complete stranger, and yet she was displaying herself to him wantonly. That gave her excitement an extra spin.

'Do you do this a lot?' he asked, his voice husky.

'Oh yes, a lot.' She opened her legs wider as she slid her hand down to the mouth of her vagina. She pushed two fingers into the wet, pliant flesh and stretched it apart like an elastic band, allowing him to see the scarlet interior. Then she pushed them inward, right up into her vagina. It was wet. She could feel it rippling. She moaned softly.

'Do you use a dildo?' he said.

'Yes,' she lied. 'But I don't need that tonight, do I, when I've got you? You are going to fuck me, aren't you?' The word made her sex convulse sharply. She used the middle finger of her other hand to play with her clitoris again, tapping it like a little hammer. This produced pinpricks of pleasure, each one lingering until they began to link up and form a much greater whole.

She was going to come, and very soon. She had never done anything like this, and she knew that it was her own daring that was exciting her quite as much as the physical sensations. She wanted the man to fuck her. And that was what it would be. Pure sex, with no complications or emotions. Just sex. That was what it had been with Matthew, after all.

'Watch me,' she said, unnecessarily, as she could see

his eyes hadn't left her sex. She was sawing her fingers in and out of her vagina as she arched her buttocks up off the bed. The expression in his eyes was total lust, his cock so erect now it sprouted vertically from his thighs, a tear of fluid escaping from the the slit. She moaned loudly, jamming her fingers deep into her sex, as her orgasm broke, wave after wave of pleasure crashing through her, each distinct and separate, each causing her whole body to shudder, her head tossed from side to side in an effort to cope with the crescendo of feeling.

'Quite a show,' he said, when she had finally slumped back on the bed.

Letitia opened her eyes. He had got to his feet, and started rolling a condom over his erection. The thin pink rubber enclosed his hard shaft, hiding all the ridges and veins, making it smooth and featureless. She wanted to tell him not to bother, that she needed to feel him riding into her without any protection, his flesh bare and rugged, his semen able to jet out into her. But she realised he thought she was a prostitute and didn't want to take a risk. A small voice in the back of her head was telling her that it was a risk for her too and was a sensible precaution, whatever her other feelings.

'Let me help,' she said, sitting up. She grabbed his erection with one hand and began licking it like the cone of an ice cream. The rubber tasted unpleasant.

'Will you come on top?' he asked.

She was there to do whatever he wanted, she reminded herself. 'I'll do anything you like, Stewart. Anything at all.' Was that true? she wondered.

Stewart lay down on the bed. 'You're very attractive, Letitia. Very. I can't believe . . .'

'You can't believe what?'

'That you're a . . .'

'Do you like this corset?' she asked, running her

hands down her sides to emphasise the dramatic curves the waspie gave her. She put one foot up on the bed and straightened a small wrinkle in one of the stockings.

'It looks sensational. And the black stockings. My wife always wears tights.'

'Is this what you want?'

Letitia kicked off her shoes and knelt on the bed. She swung one leg over his stomach and straddled his body.

'Yes.'

She saw him looking at her sex.

'Do you shave?' he asked, nodding to her short pubes.

'No, it grows that way naturally.'

He put both his hands on her thighs and caressed them, moving from the glossy sheer black nylon up to the flesh above. His left hand moved to her breasts, while his right delved between her legs. She felt his finger parting her labia and nudging up against her clit.

'It's very swollen,' he said.

'Mmm . . . that's because you've got me so excited.'

'I don't suppose I can kiss you?' he said.

She was just about to lean forward and answer his question by pressing her lips into his when she remembered that kissing was the one thing prostitutes were supposed not to allow.

'No, you cannot,' she said coquettishly.

A surge of sensation shot through her as his finger circled her clitoris. He pinched her right nipple at the same time.

'Are you going to fuck me, Stewart?' she said. 'I need it, I really do.' She was enjoying playing the role of whore. He probably thought she'd faked an orgasm just for his benefit, but it wasn't a fake at all. She reached behind her back and took hold of his erection, the rubber making it slippery. Slowly she lowered herself on her haunches until she could feel his glans nosing into her labia. The extraordinary thing was that she felt an almost unbelievable desire for him, almost as strong as the feelings Matthew had provoked. She ached for penetration.

Abandoning her cautious approach in the selection of lovers had radically changed her sexuality. She would never have believed she could have responded to this situation, here in a strange bedroom with a strange man, pretending to be a whore and dressed for the part, but she had never felt so turned on. In the past she had sometimes struggled to come once, let alone repeatedly, but now it appeared she was multi-orgasmic. She knew the feeling of his rock-hard erection pounding into her vagina would bring her off again. Her sex was already responding to the heat it was radiating into the pulpy flesh of her labia.

She squeezed his shaft hard and felt it jerk powerfully. She looked down into his face, staring straight into his eyes, then began to lower herself on to him. The wet, silky flesh of her vagina parted as the smooth rubber-covered cock slid into her. Teasing herself as much as him, she stopped when it had penetrated no more than a couple of inches, then raised herself until it was held at the mouth of her vagina again. She leant forward slightly and laid her hands on his chest. He had dark-brown nipples that were as corrugated and hard as her own. She pinched them both simultaneously, using her fingernails, and he moaned softly, his cock jerking wildly again.

'Oh, you like that, do you?' she asked.

'Yes.'

'Good.'

She slammed herself down on him, his cock rearing up into the depths of her sex, then used all her muscles to squeeze it as vigorously as she could. He moaned loudly this time.

'You're so good at this,' he said, breathily. He dropped both hands to his sides.

Letitia wriggled her hips, grinding her clitoris against the base of his phallus. It reacted with another wave of delicious sensation.

'You're going to make me come,' she said. 'Do you want to see that?'

'Of course.' He bucked his hips off the bed to try and push himself deeper.

Letitia was already on the edge of orgasm. She began to ride him, lifting herself off him then dropping down on him again, the feeling of his big sword of flesh stabbing into her creating a whole new panoply of sensations. She liked being on top, being in charge. Every three or four strokes she stopped and pressed herself down on him with all her strength, her clitoris, trapped between their bodies, throbbing violently.

Stewart raised his hands. They caressed her thighs, then moved around over her pert buttocks. He stroked the soft orbs of flesh then stretched them apart, exposing the neat circular crater of her anus. Almost immediately she felt his finger pressing against her sphincter. For a second the little muscle resisted, then gave way, and she gasped as she felt his finger wriggle its way inside. Her sex and anus contracted fiercely in unison. His finger pushed up alongside his cock, separated by the thin membranes of her body, and was generating all sorts of entirely new sensations, sensations that were as intense as anything she'd felt before. She hadn't noticed the size of his finger but it felt big, filling the little narrow passage completely. He began to pump it back and forth, at the same tempo she was using to ride up and down on him. Before she knew what was happening the initial shock of pleasure had turned inward and was triggering her orgasm, all her nerves suddenly set alight. She would never have believed her anus was capable of delivering as much pleasure as her vagina but it seemed as if they were suddenly in competition, each trying to outdo the other, each trying to make her come. But even as the waves of orgasm began to break over her, she knew it was more than that. Like the whole situation, it was the element of the forbidden, the knowledge that she had never been touched in this way before, that was bringing her off.

Losing complete control, her fingers like talons clawing at his chest, she threw her head back and screamed loudly, her breasts quivering, her whole body in stasis. As she began to relax again, the feelings ebbing away, she had an irresistible urge to kiss him. She leant forward and planted her lips on his, plunging her tongue into his mouth, the hot warmth momentarily reviving all the powerful sensations that had gone before.

'Don't tell anyone I did that,' she whispered, her lips moving against his.

She felt his finger slip from her rear. But his hands were still cupping her buttocks and pulling them apart.

'Was it tight?'

The voice was a complete shock to her. She twisted her head around to see Andrew standing in the middle of the room. He was naked apart from a light cotton robe that he was in the process of discarding. His cock, shorter but broader than Stewart's, was sticking out horizontally from his round belly.

'Perfect,' Stewart said.

'What is this?' she said. She had no idea how long Andrew had been standing watching them but she guessed it was all a carefully rehearsed plan. He had been stripped and waiting outside in the corridor with the door ajar so he could enter at the appropriate moment.

'I thought Ursula had explained, sweetie,' Andrew said. He took a little foil packet from the pocket of the robe then threw the garment aside. He came over to the foot of the bed, bending to get a better view of the bud of her anus and her sex, her labia spread thin by the breadth of Stewart's cock.

'She said you wanted to watch.' Letitia might have expected her reaction to this development to be panic or fear. Instead she was experiencing such a surge of excitement that her whole body seemed to be trembling. She could actually feel her vagina rippling against the hard cock buried inside it.

'Usually that is all I want, but you're something special, aren't you? I want a little more than that with you, sweetie. Don't worry, I'm sure Ursula will pay the extra, whatever is involved.'

Stewart was an attractive man. Andrew was not. Very definitely not. His body was flabby and weak. In other circumstances Letitia wouldn't have contemplated going to bed with him. But these were not other circumstances. Her body was simply too wired, too aroused to find the sight of him opening the condom packet and rolling the pink rubber down his hard phallus anything other than exciting.

He knelt on the bed behind her. Letitia expected Stewart to pull out to make way for Andrew, but that was not what they had in mind. Stewart's hands increased his pressure on her buttocks, pulling them further apart, and suddenly Andrew was leaning forward, his glans butting into the little puckered crater of her anus.

'No!' Letitia said with genuine alarm. She had only

been buggered once before and it wasn't an experience she had particularly enjoyed. But before she could wriggle out of the way, Andrew's stubby cock had forced its way past the initial resistance of her sphincter and was embedded in her anus.

'No,' she said in a completely different tone. The effect of having two cocks buried in her body overwhelmed her. The throbbing pain from her rear was intense, but it throbbed at exactly the same frequency as pleasure and in less than seconds had transmogrified into it, a pleasure so powerful it lanced through every nerve. This was very definitely what she had felt before.

Andrew began to move, withdrawing an inch or two, then plunging in again. As he pulled back, Stewart bucked his hips and pushed forward, the two movements carefully co-ordinated, a ballet Letitia was sure they had performed before, their cocks sliding against each other, and pulsing strongly as they did so.

Her mind was turning cartwheels. She could not believe that anything so depraved was happening to her, but it was. What was more, this twin penetration was only escalating the huge waves of sensation that threatened to drown her. Each forward thrust that Stewart made into the very top of her vagina created a nub of feeling that was immediately displaced by a similar sensation at the top of her anus, the two arcing together like electric currents. In seconds she felt an orgasm overtaking her, an orgasm so powerful it was simply on a different scale from anything she had ever felt before, wiping her clean of everything but the feeling of itself. In the distance somewhere far away she heard herself scream, a long, unnerving sound that could have been mistaken for pain just as easily as the extremes of pleasure.

The effect on the two men was obviously equally

dramatic. Almost as soon as Andrew pushed in alongside Stewart, Stewart's cock had begun to spasm. But Letitia's orgasm and the contractions it provoked in both passages of her body, firm, rhythmic contractions that gripped both phalluses and forced them together, made it impossible for him to move. As her orgasm ebbed away her vagina relaxed too, allowing him the freedom he needed. She saw his jaw clench and his eyes screw closed. His body arched up over the bed to plunge his cock as deep into her as it would go, and he remained like that, letting the pumping motion of Andrew's cock and the residual spasms of Letitia's sex bring him off. His erection jerked three or four times in rapid succession and she felt an area of warmth permeating her vagina, his spunk trapped in the thin rubber teat at the end of the condom. She moaned with regret, remembering the effect Matthew's ejaculation had had on her.

But she needn't have worried. Stewart's orgasm had been transmitted directly to Andrew. With their cocks so close it was no surprise. She felt Andrew leaning forward, his body pressed into her back. His hands wrapped themselves around her, he pushed forward one last time and his cock throbbed. She had never realised before that this final pulsing prior to ejaculation actually made the cock swell. In the pliant confines of her vagina the extra tumescence made little impact. But in the tight, narrow compass of her anus, the additional distension stretched her to the limit, causing a new wave of that particular mélange of pain and pleasure that she had experienced for the first time only moments ago. As instantly as if someone had thrown a switch, her body clenched around the two hard phalluses and another orgasm overtook her, rolling over her body like thunder clouds, darkness and lightning descending with it, the flashes of lightning huge spasms of pleasure that lit up every nerve she possessed. But even in the middle of this, even with both of the openings of her body dilated, and her orgasm roaring through her, she felt Andrew's cock kick against the walls of her anus and come too. She thought she could not possibly feel any more but this pushed her to yet another high. She could swear she could feel his sperm expanding the rubber sheath, the heat of it greater than it had been only moments before.

Slowly the two phalluses softened. As each slid from her body, both produced a spasm that made Letitia shudder with renewed pleasure.

Andrew got off his knees and sat on the edge of the bed. As she, in turn, climbed off Stewart's body, she thought she saw a look pass between them, a look of lust and desire. They had shared a woman before, she was sure, and would do so again.

Andrew began to laugh. 'I guess this means Ursula gets our order,' he said.

'I guess it does,' Stewart agreed.

Chapter Four

LETITIA PUT THE telephone down. 'He likes it. In fact, he loves it.' She jumped to her feet and ran over to Joy.

'I know, he told me.'

'He wants me to do a whole range, slip, bra, panties . . .'

'I told you. You'll have to do it in your own time, you know that, don't you? We're too busy to have you mooning around sketching all day long.'

'Don't worry. I've done a lot of work already. I can soon get the other things into shape. I'll work every evening.'

'I'm really pleased for you, Letitia,' Andrea said. She had overheard the conversation as she waited for Joy to sign off her expenses.

'Course, he might not like the other stuff.'

'You've only been here three weeks. Daniel's very fussy. It's a miracle you've got this far,' Andrea added.

'He's going to have the teddy made up. What happens then?'

'Well, he'll get some photographs done of the finished article and they'll go in the pot for the next catalogue.'

'When's that?'

'The catalogue comes out every six months. The

latest one goes to press in two weeks, so it's about four months before the presentation to decide what goes in and what doesn't.'

'So how long before I need to do the rest of the stuff?'

'Sooner the better. Then if he's got any criticisms you can do another version and still have lots of time.'

'This is great.'

Letitia sat down at her desk and tried to concentrate on the work Joy had given her. The phone rang again almost immediately.

'Letitia Drew.'

'Letitia, it's Matthew.'

'Oh.' Despite the soaring sense of elation her conversation with Daniel Travis had occasioned, the sound of Matthew's voice immediately dampened it. He was very definitely not her favourite person at the moment.

'Yes,' she said flatly.

'You're cross with me.'

'Of course I'm cross with you. What do you expect?' She lowered her voice so the rest of the people in the room couldn't hear.

'There was nothing I could do.'

'You could have warned me what she had in mind.'

'I know. But I thought . . . I thought you wanted to keep your job as much as I wanted to keep mine.'

'What exactly do you want, Matthew?' Not so long ago a phone call from Matthew Silverstone would have set her pulse racing. But at the moment she had lost all respect for the man.

'It's Ursula.' His voice sounded hesitant.

'What about her?'

'She wants to meet you for a drink.'

'What for?'

'Letitia, you know what she's like. She's got us both between a rock and a hard place. She's going to milk

88

that advantage for everything it's worth. You've got to do what she says.'

'What does she want?'

'I don't know. She wants you to meet her in the bar at the Bruniswick Hotel at seven on Friday.

'And what is it this time? Another buyer?'

'It was something you said to her, apparently.'

'Something I said?'

'I honestly don't know, Letitia, I promise you. You must know what she's like after Saturday night.'

'I do.'

'Well then. Daniel told me the news about your design. It's terrific, isn't it? You mustn't throw all that away now.'

'You mean I mustn't do anything to endanger your future.'

'Both our futures,' he said firmly. 'It was your fault as much as mine. I didn't seduce you, for Christ's sake. You were just as responsible as me.'

'I'll be there,' she said testily, and put the phone down before he had a chance to thank her.

She supposed she could always change her mind but she doubted that she would. If all her reasoned arguments for going along with the outrageous plans Ursula had made for her on Saturday night were valid, they were even more so now that she had already got her foot in the door of designing for BSL's catalogue. That was a chance she was not going to endanger.

Besides, what had happened on Saturday had left her surprisingly sanguine. She'd expected a reaction, a soul-searching and angst as to how she could have allowed herself to behave so shamefully, but on Sunday morning all she had felt was a little sore. In repose, her memories of what had happened left her not angry or resentful, but animated and exhilarated and, if she dwelt on them for too long, more than a little aroused.

In fact, the truth was she had done little else but dwell on them. She had accepted a lunch invitation to friends on Sunday and as much as she wanted to cry off through tiredness had forced herself to go. But when she returned home and flopped down in front of the television, feeling totally exhausted, the memories had flooded back to her thick and fast, every moment from the time she had stripped her clothes off in the bedroom recalled in graphic detail. She wanted to remember how she'd felt so she could file the experience away as accurately as possible for future reference. She had closed her eyes and conjured up visions of herself and the two men, making sure she remembered exactly what they had said to her and what they had done. She could picture herself lying on the bed, masturbating for Stewart, but she saw it from his point of view rather than hers, her own body on display. Similarly, when she imagined herself sandwiched between the two men, their cocks sharing her body, she saw it as if from above, a bird's-eye view that encompassed everything.

Three days had passed since then and she had been glad of a heavy workload to keep herself occupied. But at night, especially alone in bed, she had found it difficult not to go over and over what had happened and why. As far as she was concerned she had broken all the rules. If someone had told her she would be prepared to do what she had done on Saturday she would have thought them raving mad. But she had. She could have refused to co-operate when Andrew entered the room. Nor did she have the excuse that he, like Stewart, was an attractive man. She wasn't attracted to him at all. But her lust had been overwhelming and she had barely hesitated. In fact, if she was honest with herself she couldn't remember hesitating at all. She'd wanted them both.

She couldn't even hide behind the idea that she was just living out her long-term fantasy. Her fantasy, that Ursula had so graphically revived when she'd caught her in bed with Matthew, was to be watched, not to be taken simultaneously by two men.

But she did not regret it. She couldn't even say it was an experience she never wanted to repeat. Since meeting Matthew, since he had sat quietly listening to Joy Skinner interview her, her sexuality had changed. She had no idea why or wherefore but it had, dramatically. And as far as she was concerned, it was a change for the better. Now, however, her body responded with an urgency and zeal that made her previous efforts pale into insignificance. The words debauchery and depravity sprung readily to mind when she thought about what she had done, but so did rapture and ecstasy.

She supposed it might end just as suddenly and unexpectedly as it had begun, but while it lasted she decided she might as well enjoy it.

What Ursula wanted with her this time she did not know. But though she had been cross with Matthew she was more intrigued than angry. After all, the element of blackmail in Ursula's demands took away any moral imperative. She could tell herself, if she wanted an escape clause from her own lust, that she had been forced to this pass by Ursula's threats. She didn't have to take responsibility for her actions when she was merely trying to save her job. She certainly wouldn't have gone out looking for a situation like Saturday night, so the fact that she had had to cope with it for the sake of her career let her off the moral hook. At least, that was her theory.

'Letitia, can you take those swatches down to production? Adam's got a panic on again.'

'Sure thing,' she said, getting up. She went to Joy's desk and picked up the latest samples of the materials they were using in two new lines. Soon, she thought to herself, if she could come up with the goods, it might well be her line of lingerie BSL was manufacturing.

The Bruniswick Hotel was new and very expensive, and in a premier position overlooking Hyde Park. It had a flaming gas flambeau on either side of its entrance, with a large sweeping driveway where a fleet of Rolls Royces, Ferraris and Aston Martins had been valet-parked by the uniformed commissionaires.

'Good evening, madam,' one of them said, holding the big glass door open as Letitia walked up to it.

'Good evening,' she said, smiling. 'Where's the bar?'

'Straight ahead, madam, right down to the end. You can't miss it.'

He was right. Letitia walked the length of the foyer and found herself in a large, cavernous room with a polished wood floor and a long, snake-like bar made from stainless steel. Behind the bar, glass shelves backed by opaque cream perspex displayed antique bottles of various spirits.

Sitting at one of the ultra-modern bar stools, a tripod of stainless steel supporting a thick dark-blue leather cushion, Ursula Silverstone was sipping a cocktail. She was wearing a leopardskin print suit over a tight cream body. Her high-heeled shoes were leopardskin print too, and her legs were sheathed in champagne-coloured nylon.

'Hi,' she said as Letitia approached. 'Glad you could make it,' she added with heavy irony.

Letitia had decided to be a little more daring with her

clothes in such a swanky establishment and had chosen a short cinnamon-coloured dress in a glittery material with a straight-across neckline. Its thin straps extended up to her neck then crossed over at the back, rejoining the dress at the side of the bodice. It left most of her back and her shoulders bare, and Letitia had pinned her long hair into a tight chignon to emphasise the fact. The dress made a statement. She wanted Ursula to know that she was not intimidated.

'Good evening,' Letitia said coolly, climbing up on to an adjacent barstool. She was wearing dark-brown slingback high heels, and flesh-coloured nylon, the skirt of the dress long enough to conceal the fact that they were BSL's own hold-ups.

'Don't you look lovely?' Ursula said, adding, 'A drink?'

'What's that?' Letitia asked, pointing to the triangular-shaped glass on the bar in front of Ursula.

'Gin martini.'

'I'll have one of those.'

Ursula signalled to the barman and conveyed in sign language what she wanted.

'You really are a beautiful woman, aren't you? I can see why Matthew was so interested.'

'As I understand it, Matthew has been interested in a lot of women,' Letitia said. She had thought a lot about what she intended to say tonight. 'I'm not the only one.'

Ursula smiled. 'Oh, you're not the first. I know that. I'm sure you won't be the last.'

'So why do you stay with him?'

The barman arrived with a cocktail shaker. He shook it vigorously then laid out two white coasters bearing an elaborately designed B, the Bruniswick's hotel logo, on which he placed two cocktail glasses. They had been in the freezer and were now frosted with condensation.

He poured the cocktails from the shaker then added a twist of lemon.

'Thank you,' Ursula said, as she finished her first drink and allowed him to take the glass away. 'Cheers,' she said to Letitia.

Letitia picked up her own glass. 'Cheers.'

'So why do I stay with him? Because it is convenient. Because he is an excellent lover, as you know. And besides, while the mouse is away, the cat can play.' She smiled, that thin smile Letitia had seen before, her fleshy lips pulled tight.

'Why do you care what he does then?'

'I told you. He has been neglecting me. I like to play away from home but I like to play at home too. That's what we always had. Recently he's been showing signs of fatigue. To put it crudely, I'm not having him servicing you while I'm sitting at home twiddling my thumbs.'

'Wouldn't it be easier if you went your separate ways?'

'I'm not going to give him up.' She sipped her drink. 'My two friends were most impressed, incidentally. I got my order. They kept asking me for your telephone number so they could book a return engagement. I gather you were most . . . accommodating.'

'I didn't have much choice.' She had no intention of telling Ursula her real feelings about the experience.

Ursula laughed. 'I thought the punishment fitted the crime, didn't you?'

'Is that what I'm here for?'

'A few years ago, when I was building up my business, I was trying to get my clothes into a new chain of boutiques. It was run by a German woman. She was gorgeous, blond with this incredibly long, thick hair. It seemed to shine. Well, she invited me to her house for dinner one night. I thought it was perfectly innocent.'

After what Matthew had told her, Letitia could guess what was coming. 'But it wasn't.'

'No. I discovered that she was very happy to give me a large order provided I went to bed with her.'

'And?'

'I had never been to bed with a woman before.' Letitia saw Ursula's eyes turn inward for a moment. 'She was very good at it.' She suddenly looked straight at Letitia. 'Have you ever been to bed with a woman?'

'No.'

'But you were prepared to?'

'What do you mean?'

'Last Saturday. Isn't that what you said? That you thought I wanted to take you to bed?'

'And that's why I'm here?'

'Yes. I thought it would be fun to explore our mutual attraction.'

'What makes you think it was mutual?'

'Oh, come on, Letitia. We both felt it. You may not have had any experience but you were just as turned on when you kissed me as I was.'

However much Letitia had tried to kid herself and make up excuses to deny it, she knew it was true. She sipped her drink and tried to sort out her feelings.

'Which is why you'd convinced yourself I'd invited you to my house to have sex with you. And why, I imagine, you'd decided you were going to agree.'

Though the barman was at the other end of the bar, Letitia thought he'd overheard the last remark. He started inching closer, polishing glasses as he did so.

'I didn't have any choice. I still don't.'

Ursula smiled broadly this time. She had large white teeth. She ran her tongue around her bottom lip. 'How true. Did you see Piers Green on television last week?

Quite a performance. He appears to think that men are much too quick to ignore their marriage vows and that most women are flaunting themselves, presumably in BSL lingerie. As he was happily married for thirty years, he imagines everyone should be the same. Especially . . .' she sipped her drink, '. . . the people who work for him.'

'How did he come to own a lingerie company? Black Stockings Lingerie is hardly the right image for him, is it?'

'Black Stockings was owned by another group. He bought the group out, and was going to sell Black Stockings on until he found out how good the profits are. That doesn't mean he wouldn't change his mind if there was any hint of scandal.'

'You don't have to convince me,' Letitia said. 'I want to keep my job.'

Ursula put her hand on Letitia's knee. 'Good. Shall we go then?'

'Go where?'

'You'll see.'

'Don't make me do this, Ursula.' Letitia suddenly felt apprehensive.

'Why not? You want it as much as I do.' Ursula's eyes looked straight into hers.

Letitia simply could not think of a reply to that. Could she deny it? At that exact moment she actually didn't know what she wanted.

As the barman was now no more than two feet away, it was not difficult to attract his attention. He brought a bill and Ursula left a twenty-pound note without glancing at it.

They climbed down from the stools and walked out of the bar and across the foyer, their high-heeled shoes clacking on the hardwood floor. But instead of heading out of the hotel, Ursula turned left towards a bank of lifts.

'I booked a room,' she said, by way of explanation.

Letitia found her heart pounding. She had imagined they would be taking a taxi back to Ursula's house, which would give her time to calm herself down. But if Ursula had a room it was only going to be a matter of minutes before she was faced with a reality that was in a way far more challenging than anything that had happened so far. Last Saturday she had wound her courage up to the idea that Ursula might want to explore a sexual agenda; now it appeared that was exactly what she was going to do. What was more difficult for her to come to terms with was whether she wanted it too.

They got into the lift and Ursula pressed the button for the sixth floor.

'Why not your house?' Letitia asked.

'I like hotels. Give me your hand.'

Ursula took her hand before Letitia could respond, then brought it up to her lips. She kissed the palm, then the inside of the fingers, then sucked the tips of her fingers into her mouth. Letitia shuddered, every nerve in her body set on edge.

The lift doors opened and a middle-aged couple stood looking in. The woman, in a bright floral dress, blushed. 'Sorry, we're going down,' she said, shuffling off to one side.

The doors closed again.

On the sixth floor Ursula led the way along the corridor, its dark-green carpet a thick Wilton. She stopped outside Room 656 and inserted a thin plastic card into the computer lock. The door sprang open.

'After you,' she said.

Letitia walked inside. In fact, the room was a suite,

the sitting room large and spacious with a view over Hyde Park. The walls were decorated in pink silk and the carpet was red. There were two sofas, a desk and a large television and video recorder as well as a sideboard containing a minibar.

'Do you want another drink?' Ursula asked.

'No.'

'Good.'

Ursula came up behind Letitia, pressing her body into her back. She wrapped her arms around Letitia's waist and kissed her shoulder so gently it felt like a butterfly had landed there. The palm of her left hand flitted across the glittery material of Letitia's dress and circled her nipples one after the other. They stiffened immediately, producing a hard pulse of feeling that took Letitia completely by surprise. Her skin pimpled into goose bumps. Ursula's lips touched Letitia's neck, this time sucking on the flesh, then quite suddenly she pulled away.

'All right, you can go,' Ursula said firmly.

'What!'

'You can go. Leave.' She walked over to the window and stared out at the view. 'You're right, I can't make you do this.'

'What do you mean?'

'Go, Letitia. Don't you understand English? I made a mistake, all right. I can't blackmail you into doing this. You'd better go before I change my mind,' she said without looking around.

Letitia's heart was beating like a drum and she was short of breath. 'And if I don't want to go?'

Ursula turned around slowly. 'Why would you want to stay?' Her eyes were staring at Letitia, glinting like two chips of diamond.

'Isn't that obvious?'

'You'll have to explain it to me.'

'I want to stay because I want to go to bed with you,' Letitia said calmly. And it was absolutely true. She knew what she wanted now, her ambivalence gone. Her whole body was tingling, and deep in her sex she felt the unmistakable stirrings of lust. She could still feel Ursula's lips on her neck and her nipples were as hard as pebbles. Before Ursula had found her with Matthew in the company flat, the idea of having sex with a woman had never occurred to her. But that brief encounter had changed all that. Though she had convinced herself that the only reason she was prepared to sleep with Ursula was to save her job, faced with the fact that it was no longer necessary, she had to admit that was not her only motivation. Whatever had happened to her sexuality in the last weeks, whatever awakening had occurred, it appeared she still needed to test and explore its outer limits.

Letitia moved towards Ursula, wanting to take the initiative. Boldly, she raised her hand and ran it under Ursula's jacket to her left breast. She cupped the warm, pliant flesh, feeling the hard nipple against her palm. Slowly leaning forward, she brushed her lips against Ursula's mouth. Ursula did not move, allowing her to pursue her own ends. Letitia's tongue licked her lower lip, then pushed very tentatively between them. Ursula's mouth was hot and wet. She felt her gently sucking her tongue in, then pressing her own against it. Ursula's arm snaked around Letitia's waist and suddenly the tempo changed, the kiss becoming passionate, their lips mashed together, their tongues entwined.

Letitia felt a surge of pleasure. She wriggled her body against Ursula, amazed at how different it felt, the planes and angles of a woman's figure completely different from a man. Strangest of all was the absence of male genitalia, the hot, hard shaft that usually made its presence felt as she kissed a man. Instead she felt the flatness of Ursula's stomach and her pubic bone grinding into her own. With one hand still squeezing Ursula's breast, she ran the other over her back and down to her small, neat bottom. As she caressed it she could feel the silky material of her skirt rubbing against the equally slick cream body she was wearing underneath it, and that was another new sensation, her hand moulding itself to the curves and yielding softness of her buttocks.

She broke the kiss. 'You'll have to help me. I don't know what to do,' she said seriously. If she had any doubt about her ability to respond to a woman it had disappeared. Her body was reacting with all the familiar signs of arousal, her clitoris throbbing and her sex moist.

'Come in here,' Ursula said.

She took Letitia's hand and led her through to the bedroom. The room was only slightly smaller than the one they had left, with pale-primrose-coloured walls and brightly patterned yellow and blue curtains. There was a huge double bed, its counterpane neatly folded back. The curtains had already been drawn across the large window.

'Do you want to use the bathroom?' Ursula asked. There were two doors to the right of the bed and one of them was ajar. Beyond, Letitia could see a bathroom tiled in greyish marble.

'No.'

Ursula took off her jacket. She reached behind her back and unzipped her skirt, then let it fall to the floor. The legs of the cream body were cut so high on the hip they revealed the sides of her pelvis under the sheer nylon of her tights. The gusset of the body was narrow and had creased where it folded into her sex. The material was tight and flattened her breasts back against her chest slightly, her small puckered nipples outlined clearly under it.

Letitia could still feel her heart thumping against her ribs. She had taken a real risk with herself on Saturday night and had no regrets, but this felt a hundred times more dangerous. Which didn't mean she was getting cold feet. Quite the reverse. Now Ursula had removed the threat of blackmail, what she was doing was entirely of her own volition, making her feel daring and in control. That, in turn, enhanced her physical excitement.

In this spirit she took hold of the hem of her dress and pulled it over her head. As the dress was practically backless, she wasn't wearing a bra, her only underwear BSL's shimmering hold-ups, and a pair of black silk panties, another of the company's creations. They were no more than two chevrons of black stretched tightly across her navel and her buttocks.

'You've got a beautiful body,' Ursula said, almost to herself. 'Sit on the bed.'

Letitia obeyed. She watched as Ursula reached down between her own legs and unclipped the three fasteners that held the gusset of the cream body in place. She pulled it up over her head and threw it aside. Her big breasts trembled, the skin wrinkled by the constriction of the tight material.

Ursula knelt at Letitia's feet. She picked up her left foot and eased off her shoe, then stooped slightly and kissed her toes through the shiny nylon. She licked the arch of her foot then slipped the toes into her mouth and sucked them hard, her eyes looking up Letitia's long leg to where the tight welt at the top of the stocking dimpled her thigh, the black silk gusset above pulled taut across her sex. Ursula allowed the left foot to drop, then picked up the right and followed the same procedure, except this time her mouth moved upwards, kissing and licking and sucking at the flesh of Letitia's calf, then moving up over her knee.

'Lie back,' Ursula said, the pitch of her voice distinctly lower.

Letitia did so. She felt Ursula's mouth begin to move further up, creating delicious trills of pleasure. As it reached the naked flesh above the stocking top, Letitia gasped, the contrast between the clothed and the unclothed contact extreme. Her whole body was so sensitised she was sure she could feel Ursula's hot breath playing against the silk of her panties.

The mouth left her thigh. Her legs were lifted, one by one, and placed over Ursula's shoulders so her bottom was raised slightly and her sex angled up. Then the mouth was back again, sucking at the long sinews of her thighs and making Letitia moan again.

Letitia closed her eyes. Immense waves of excitement were already rolling over her. She felt Ursula's finger insinuating under the elasticated leg of the panties and pulling them to one side, and was sure her labia pulsed as they were exposed. Then she felt the most delicate of touches, a kiss like the way Ursula had kissed her shoulder when they'd first come into the suite, her lips barely brushing against Letitia's pouting sex. The lips were replaced by her tongue. With just as subtle a contact, it slid down the right side of Letitia's sex, flitted over her puckered anus, then licked along the left side, carefully avoiding, or so it seemed, all contact with the more intimate flesh. Letitia's labia contracted sharply as if trying to draw attention to themselves, but Ursula ignored them, her tongue working up along the crease

102

of her pelvis. It followed the leg of the panties right up to Letitia's hip, then started across her belly.

'Please,' Letitia breathed, crossing her ankles over Ursula's back so her thighs were spread further apart.

Immediately Ursula's mouth descended, across the wrinkled black silk of the panties and down over the short soft hair of Letitia's mons. Her tongue prodded into the fourchette at the top of Letitia's labia and butted against her clit. Letitia felt an enormous rush of pleasure sweep over her. Instead of flicking the little button back and forth, Ursula seemed to flatten her tongue against it, pushing it back against Letitia's pubic bone. She relaxed the pressure slightly, then alternated between hardness and softness, using that to create a sensation of rhythm.

Letitia had never felt anything like this before. Ursula's tongue was generating heat that, in combination with the undulating pressure, made her clitoris throb wildly. But just as this new sensation was flowing through her body, it was joined by another. She felt Ursula's finger slip between her labia. It found the mouth of her vagina and began to circle the opening, stretching the malleable and very wet flesh but not penetrating it. The nerves clustered there registered approval with a sharp shock of pleasure which rapidly turned to a measured pulse centred in the depths of her vagina.

Her body was on fire, the flames lapping at all her erogenous zones, her nipples so hard they felt as if they had been knotted, her sex so wet she could feel her juices running out of her. But the physical sensations that Ursula's artful mouth and fingers were creating were matched by what was going on in Letitia's mind. It was the element of the forbidden, of breaking a taboo, that was adding piguancy to what she felt, the fact that

103

it was a woman not a man who was doing this to her reinforced by every sense. The smell of Ursula's expensive perfume, the feel of Ursula's soft, silky skin, her auburn hair sweeping across Letitia's thighs, were all things she had never experienced before. But most of all it was the way Ursula was caressing her which was so completely different from a man. Men had performed the same service, even in the same position, with her legs hooked over their shoulders and her heels digging into their backs, but it had never felt like this.

Two new elements entered the equation of passion. First she felt Ursula's hand snaking up her body to grasp her breast. It squeezed it hard, then took hold of her nipple and pulled her breast up by it, stretching the flesh into a pyramid, and making it throb quite as strongly as her clit already was. Then down between her legs another of Ursula's fingers began to probe the little hole of her anus. It adopted the same strategy as its companion, not penetrating beyond the opening, but circling it, pulling the puckered flesh this way and that.

Letitia had barely been aware of how sensitive this part of her anatomy could be; but it appeared, since Saturday night, that all that had changed dramatically. Now it responded as articulately as the rest of her sex, with its own vocabulary of delight.

There was no slow build-up, no gathering momentum as the waves of pleasure reached a climax, but a sudden and enormous pulse of feeling that hit Letitia like a flash of lightning, arched her body off the bed and dumped it back down again unceremoniously, quivering under the impact, her thighs clenched around Ursula's head.

'Oh God, what did you do to me?' She lifted her head and looked down at Ursula.

'You're just very responsive,' she said, smiling. She

gently moved her fingers away from Letitia's sex, though not without producing a reaction that made the blonde's body quake.

Letitia lifted her legs from Ursula's shoulders and scrambled up the bed. She hooked her thumbs into the waistband of her panties and raised her buttocks so she could pull them over her hips. Her chignon had started to escape from its pins, so she sat up and began pulling them out, letting her long hair fall down her back. She shook her head and combed her fingers through her hair.

Letitia was struggling with the implications of what had happened. She had expected that her response to a woman's touch might be agreeable, even passionate, but she had not anticipated that it would be so violent and fiery. She had been motivated by curiosity, by a desire to explore the feelings that she had only recently tried to deny, but judging from her reaction, Ursula had tapped into a streak of her sexuality that she had successfully hidden even from herself. Had she not recently had such explosive orgasms with men – and men in the plural, literally – she would have begun to worry about whether her predilection over the years, when she had toiled at heterosexual sex with only moderate rewards, had been misdirected. As it was, she found it hard to understand how she could have reacted so boisterously to both genders.

This wasn't the time to work on that problem, however, she decided.

'I want you now,' she said unabashed.

Ursula got to her feet. Quickly she skimmed her tights down her legs, then sat on the edge of the bed.

'What do I do?' Letitia said. Her sex was still alive, squirming with deliciously sensuous trills of feeling.

'Exactly what I just did to you.'

105

Ursula twisted around on the bed. She slid her hand around Letitia's neck and kissed her full on the mouth, her tongue darting between her lips. She twisted her head from side to side, crushing their lips together as their nipples jiggled against each other. Without breaking the kiss, she slowly lowered Letitia back on to the bed until her head was resting on the pillow. Then, as she came up on to her knees, she ran her mouth down Letitia's neck, sucking and kissing her throat, while her hands gathered the blonde's breasts, pushing them up and together, their nipples pointing at the ceiling. Her mouth sucked on them one by one, then she nipped them both with her teeth.

'I want you,' Letitia repeated. 'Please . . .'

Ursula swung her thigh over Letitia's hips, presenting her with a close-up view of her tight, pert buttocks. Then she began to walk backwards on her knees until her sex was poised above Letitia's face. Her sex was small and neat, her labia thin and hairless. They were open too, and Letitia could see the glistening scarlet flesh they protected.

Eagerly Letitia hooked her hands around Ursula's thighs, and levered her head off the bed. She hesitated for a moment, not through any lack of desire but because she wanted to take time to savour the moment, to realise that this was the first time she had ever done this to a woman. That thought made her clitoris spasm powerfully against her own labia. Ursula's perfume had combined with another more primitive scent, producing a heady aroma. Letitia inhaled deeply, then planted her lips firmly on Ursula's sex and kissed it as if it were a mouth, her tongue dipping into the sticky honey pot.

Ursula gasped as Letitia pulled her down on to her face. With her head resting against the pillow Letitia moved her tongue up the slit of Ursula's sex until she found her clitoris. She had no idea what to expect. The only clitoris she had ever felt was her own, and that only with her finger. Ursula's clit felt smaller but harder, a tiny lozenge-shaped pebble. Immediately Letitia pressed her tongue against it, doing exactly what Ursula had done to her. But after a moment or two of that, she adopted a different tactic, using the tip of her tongue to burrow all around the little button as if trying to find a way inside. She felt Ursula's whole body shudder as she did this, her buttocks clenching and her labia, pressed tightly against Letitia's chin, pulsing strongly.

'Yes,' Ursula moaned.

Letitia worked her right hand down over Ursula's buttocks. She pushed her middle finger into the neat mouth of her vagina and began circumnavigating the rim just as Ursula had done to her. Again, almost instantly, she felt Ursula's body tense, the muscles of her thighs hardening, raising and lowering herself almost imperceptibly on her haunches.

Then she was aware of something else. Ursula's hands were pushing her thighs apart. As she co-operated and spread her legs, Ursula bent forward and pressed her mouth to Letitia's sex, her tongue finding her clitoris with unerring accuracy.

Suddenly everything changed. It was like a chain reaction. The feeling of Ursula's tongue once again performing its unfamiliar dance against her clit sent Letitia into a spasm of pleasure. And, as her mouth and tongue were so intimately linked to Ursula's body, her reaction, the hot exhaust of pleasure that escaped her mouth, was communicated instantly to Ursula, whose body responded in the same way. And so it went on, a helix of pleasure that spiralled higher and higher, their bodies locked in the same rhythm, experiencing the same sensations.

107

Letitia knew she was coming, but the fact that Ursula was coming too, the fact that she could feel the other woman's orgasm building almost as acutely as she could feel her own, just doubled everything she felt.

There, in a strange hotel room, they clung to each other, their bodies joined as if they had been welded together. Letitia had noticed the direct connection between her mouth and her sex before, but here it was more complicated. Certainly the wetness and heat her sex was generating was mirrored in her mouth. But this time her mouth was melting into another woman's sex as well and she could feel everything it was feeling, the heat and wetness and throbbing passion they both produced like nothing she had felt before.

It was impossible to tell who came first. As Letitia felt Ursula's clitoris jerking wildly against her tongue, her own went into spasm too and the spiralling sensations tightened into one single whole. At the top of the spiral, Letitia's nerves swirled in a vortex of pleasure as extreme as anything she had felt before. It paralysed her, every muscle locked around the central core of ecstasy, a deep, dark passion.

And then, like a bank of clouds moving in front of the sun, the mood changed. As Ursula rolled off her, Letitia heard a voice.

'Quite a performance.'

'She loves it.'

'I can see that.'

Letitia opened her eyes. Matthew Silverstone was standing at the foot of the bed. He was naked, his fist wrapped around his erection, his foreskin already pulled back, the smooth pink acorn of his glans exposed.

It was Matthew's presence that had cast the dark shadow over her emotions. Letitia couldn't understand what he was doing there. It was probably another of Ursula's little games but she couldn't understand why he hadn't told her this was the plan. She had the strange feeling that there was something more to it than that, something sinister and underhand. She wanted time to think and work out all the implications, but there was no time. She couldn't do anything but respond to the aching need the sight of his cock had created. She wanted him. After the tantalising orgasms she had experienced on the soft mouth of a woman, what she wanted more than she had ever wanted anything in her life was the hot hardness of a man.

'Are you going to fuck me?' she said, hoping he would find her debauched abandon irresistible. She could see he was looking at her sex, her sticky juices leaking on to the sheet, and she angled it up at him, wanting to show him how it needed him.

She got what she wanted. He vaulted on to the bed and pulled himself on top of her. His cock plunged right into her vagina, hardly grazing her labia, her wetness making the penetration frictionless. With more urgency than she had ever felt in any man, he was driving up into her, his thrusts so strong and powerful they lifted her buttocks off the bed. She felt his glans thrusting against the neck of her womb, her vagina completely filled by him, her clitoris hammered by the base of his cock.

Before she could think or do anything, before she could wrap her arms around him, before she could even gasp with pleasure, she felt herself being sucked down into orgasm again, down into that dark pit of ultimate pleasure. This time her whole body was shuddering, her head tossed from side to side, her sex clenching convulsively around the hard muscle that invaded it, her limbs stretched out as though on a medieval rack, every sinew in her body as taut as piano wire.

The rest was like a dream. It was performed in slow motion. She opened her eyes to see Ursula kneeling by her side.

'You know what we agreed,' she said to her husband.

Matthew had stopped his relentless pounding, withdrew from her sex, though she was too numb to feel it, and knelt between her outstretched legs.

Ursula reached forward, took his cock in her fist and began to pump her hand up and down. In three or four strokes his glans, projecting from the top of her fingers, swelled and jerked violently, and white semen jetted out of him in a long parabolic arc, eventually spattering down on Letitia's naked body, over her belly and her breasts.

Ursula immediately leant forward and began to lick it up, Matthew watching her every movement avidly.

'We must do this again,' he said, his mouth breaking into a broad grin.

Chapter Five

LETITIA COULDN'T SLEEP. A thunderstorm had been rolling around the city since the small hours, but the echoing claps of thunder were not the reason she lay awake, tossing and turning, throwing the covers off then dragging them back on again, alternately hot and cold. It was the fact that she was angry.

Ursula and Matthew had planned it together. Everything that had happened. 'You know what we agreed.' Wasn't that what Ursula had said? The whole evening had been set up for their mutual pleasure. She had no idea how long Matthew had been watching them or how he'd got into the room without her noticing, but that had obviously been planned too. Perhaps he'd been hiding in the wardrobe. Or the suite had another bedroom. There was, she remembered, a second door alongside the bathroom. Admittedly Ursula had given her the free choice to leave before anything had happened, but in retrospect that appeared more like a cheap trick, like a magician offering a dupe the chance to choose a card when, in fact, the choice was predetermined. Ursula had known that she would stay.

The point was that Ursula had told her husband exactly what she was going to do and arranged for him to be there to witness it and then to take part. And that made Letitia wonder if everything, right from the moment Ursula had burst into the company flat and pretended to be outraged, hadn't all been a set-up, manufactured with the purpose of ensnaring her in a trap so she could be manipulated to their purposes.

That wasn't to say she regretted what she had done. Far from it. What she had experienced last night had been another lesson in just how receptive and responsive her body could be. The idea that her rather lacklustre sexual encounters in the past came from some inner failing, some psychological or even physical lack, had been completely and utterly dispelled. Whatever their motivations, the Silverstones – singly and jointly – had completely changed her attitude to sex. They had empowered her, allowed her to see that sex was not just something that was done to her, but could be controlled and ordered to suit her own needs. And they had helped define what those needs were.

But despite all that, she felt used. And trapped. Ursula had made it very clear she intended to use her again. The withdrawal of her threat had only been temporary. She was planning a little party at her house next Saturday, she'd told her. If Letitia wanted to keep her job she would be there. Matthew had once again begged his wife to let her off the hook, but this time his pleadings had sounded hollow and insincere. Nor had his wife threatened him again this time. The more she thought about it, the more Letitia was convinced he had been instrumental in getting her into this position, and the more angry she became. She even wondered whether she was the first; if this was a routine they had practised with the other girls he'd seduced, as a way of feeding Ursula's taste for bisexuality.

Finally giving up the effort to get to sleep, as a clap of thunder echoed almost overhead, Letitia got out of bed and went to the kitchen to fetch a glass of milk. She didn't put the lights on but sat at her kitchen table gazing out at the panoramic view of the London skyline her fifth-floor flat provided, as lightning forked across the horizon.

As well as her dark thoughts about how she was being used, Letitia was trying to work out how she felt about having had sex with a woman for the first time. It had been thrilling. There was no point in denying that. But for all the thrills and excitement, what Ursula had introduced her to had left her feeling uneasy. Perhaps after years of strictly heterosexual sex she was not ready to admit to herself that she could get real sexual satisfaction from a woman. Perhaps she was afraid of turning into an aggressive bull dyke with slicked-back short hair and a man's suit. She did not know. It was something that was going to take time to come to terms with.

There was one thing she did know, however. Despite the wild flights of passion she had experienced last night, she was determined not to be used again. At any price. Exploring her sexuality was not an excuse for allowing herself to be demeaned. She liked her job at BSL, but she decided emphatically that she was simply not prepared to be manipulated and blackmailed any more. Whether Ursula was acting alone, or was in league with her husband, in the end made no difference. After what she had arranged with Stewart and Andrew there was no telling what her 'little party' would involve. It was not that Letitia no longer wished to visit the wilder shores of sexual experience or was tiring of exploring the many facets of her own sexual feelings; but she wanted to do it on her own terms, not someone else's. She supposed she should never have allowed herself to be sucked into Ursula's schemes in the first place, but now it was time to draw a line in the sand.

As she finished her milk and went back to bed, her anger evaporated and depression set in. If Matthew was in on his wife's schemes, she was sure he would find some excuse to fire her once she told him she was no longer prepared to play ball. She was still on her two-month probationary period so she very much doubted she would have a case for unfair dismissal, but even if she did, it would not make up for losing her job. And if Ursula was acting alone, then both she and Matthew would be out on the street. Either way, her career at BSL would be over.

On Monday morning she arrived at work especially early. As she had thought, the offices were deserted. She flew up to Jackie's office on the first floor and sat at her desk. Fortunately it was not locked and Letitia found what she was looking for in the bottom drawer, where green hanging dividers suspended in a rack held a number of what were obviously her most frequently used files. One was clearly labelled *Piers Green*.

Letitia took the file out. It contained letters from Matthew Silverstone reporting on various financial developments. Quickly she copied down Piers Green's office and home addresses and the telephone number of the private line in his office.

It had come to her at five a.m. She'd had an idea. The best means of defence was attack. She wasn't going to lose her job at BSL without a fight. Rather than waiting for Ursula to visit Piers Green and dish the dirt, wouldn't it be better if she went to him herself and confessed all? There was no doubt about his views on the subject of adultery, but perhaps if she told him what Ursula had done, he might not be so quick to condemn her own involvement. It was at least worth a try, she thought.

At lunchtime she went to the telephone box on the corner of the street and dialled the number.

'Piers Green's office, how may I help?' The female voice was brisk and efficient.

'I'd like to make an appointment to see Mr Green, please.'

'I'm sorry, Mr Green is out of the country until Thursday. May I ask who's calling?'

'My name is Drew, Letitia Drew.'

'And may I ask what this is in connection with?'

'Black Stockings Lingerie. I need to talk to him about a personal matter.'

'I'm sorry, Ms Drew, Mr Green is a very busy man. Perhaps you'd be better discussing it with the MD of that company . . .' she paused a moment as if looking it up, '. . . a Mr Matthew Silverstone.'

'It's Mr Silverstone that I need to talk to Mr Green about.'

'Oh, in that case I would suggest you write a letter explaining exactly what the problem is. We'll see it is dealt with. Mr Green does not deal with the day-to-day running of any of his companies, Ms Drew.'

'But he will be back on Thursday?'

'Yes. Goodbye.'

The dialling tone erupted in Letitia's ear. She put the phone down in disgust. She had been stupid. How could she have imagined that a man like Piers Green was going to drop everything to see her? His secretary was employed to make sure he wasn't bothered by an endless queue of people wanting to take up his valuable time.

Letitia smiled, not at all discouraged. She would have to think of another way.

On Thursday she had dressed for the part. A stretchy red dress, with three-quarter-length sleeves and a scoop neck, that clung to her firm bust, narrow waist and flared hips, its extremely short skirt displaying Letitia's long slender legs sheathed in shimmering BSL flesh-coloured tights. Spiky red high-heeled shoes gave shape and definition to her calves and a distinct pout to her bottom. Red was the best colour with her long blonde hair, which she had brushed out over her back. She had changed in the toilet at work, fending off Joy's questions as to where she was going by telling her she had a date.

The taxi dropped her outside Liverpool Street Station and she walked across the road to an imposing office block, its black glass windows mirroring the activity on the street. A semi-circular smoked-glass canopy supported on an elaborate steel frame jutted out above the main entrance where twin revolving doors were already starting to disgorge employees on to the street.

Letitia took up position on the corner of the building and glanced at her watch. It was six fifteen. At five fifteen she had rung Piers Green's office saying that she was Matthew Silverstone's secretary and Mr Silverstone wanted to send him an urgent fax. Was Mr Green in his office or at home? The brisk and efficient female voice had told her he was in his office and would not be going home until six thirty. Letitia opened her handbag and took out the picture she had photocopied in her lunch hour at the local library taken from last month's edition of the *Economist*. Piers Green was a man of sixty-two, slender and immaculately groomed, with a full head of completely white hair. He would not be difficult to recognise.

At six twenty-five a highly polished claret Rolls-Royce Silver Wraith drew up outside the building. The chauffeur got out of the car, leant against the the bonnet, took out his copy of the *Daily Mirror* and began to read. Letitia moved a little closer to the revolving doors. Luckily the windows on the ground floor were not opaque and she could see into the vast marbled lobby of the building. At six thirty-seven the stainless-steel doors of one of a bank of three lifts opened and Piers Green appeared, wearing a beautifully tailored navy suit, a white shirt and a dark-blue silk tie. He strode over to the nearest of the revolving doors.

Letitia timed it perfectly. As Piers emerged from the revolving door, the chauffeur opened the passenger door of the Rolls. Letitia got just ahead of Piers as he marched to the car, and slipped into the spacious interior one step ahead of him, sliding across the leather seat to the far side.

' 'Ere, what do you think you're playing at?' the chauffeur protested. If it hadn't been for his boss blocking his way, he would have climbed into the car and hauled her out. But Piers was busy examining the unexpected passenger, taking a great interest in her long shapely legs.

'I'm sorry Mr Green, but I just had to speak to you,' she said.

'Just you get out of there,' the chauffeur roared as he ran around to the other side of the car.

'It's all right, Fred,' Piers said calmly. 'Let's see what she has to say for herself.' He climbed into the car beside Letitia, his eyes firmly rooted on her legs. 'Good evening, young lady,' he said.

'Good evening.'

'So what is this all about?'

The chauffeur reluctantly got behind the wheel.

There was a glass partition between the front and rear of the car which was wound down.

'This is personal,' Letitia said.

'Of course. Fred, you can take me home. I'm sure we can drop this young lady off somewhere on the way.'

'Yes, sir,' the chauffeur replied.

Piers pressed a button in the little console set into the walnut veneer at the side of his seat, and the glass divider closed with a whirr of electric motors and a satisfying clunk.

'Would you like a drink?'

The interior of the car had everything. There was a small television, a video recorder, a telephone on either side of the central armrest and a walnut cocktail cabinet mounted over the transmission tunnel.

'No thank you.'

'I make it a habit to have a glass of single malt on my way home. A very good single malt. A little tradition. Won't you join me?'

'If you insist.'

'But I do.'

As the car moved out into the traffic, he leant forward and opened the cocktail cabinet. Inside was a tantalus containing three square crystal decanters and six crystal tumblers set in circular walnut-veneered glass holders. Piers poured the amber-coloured whisky.

'Cheers, my dear.'

'Cheers.'

A little self-consciously, not having expected this response, Letitia sipped the malt. It was delicious.

'So, my dear, what makes you adopt such an unorthodox way of approaching me? Not that it wasn't perfectly charming.' He gazed down at her knees, the sheen of the nylon catching the light.

'I work for Black Stockings Lingerie, sir,' she said.

'Oh, please call me Piers. And your name is?'

'Letitia Drew.'

'Go on, Ms Drew. You work for Matthew Silverstone?'

'That's right. Look, this is really embarrassing. Do you mind if I'm frank with you?'

'I would prefer it.'

'Matthew and I had an affair. I can't pretend I didn't know what I was doing. I mean, I knew he was married.'

'I see.' His tone of voice appeared unchanged by the news.

'Well, his wife found out about it.'

'Ursula?'

'Yes. She told me, well, us, that if we did not do exactly what she wanted she would tell you about it.'

'And why should she want to do that?'

Letitia tried to read the expression on his face but it remained unruffled.

'She seemed to think that we would both be dismissed out of hand.'

'Oh dear.' He chuckled. 'I can imagine why. My reputation precedes me.'

'You've made a lot of speeches about adultery.'

He smiled and sipped his whisky. 'It's true, I have. Now tell me, my dear, what exactly did she want you to do?'

'That's the point. That's why I had to come and see you. I know what I did was wrong in your eyes. It was probably wrong in my eyes too. I'd never, ever had an affair with a married man before. There was just something about Matthew.'

'He's very attractive to women, isn't he?' Piers said sympathetically.

'Yes. Yes, he is. He was to me, at least.'

'And what did she ask you to do?'

'She wanted me to go to bed with two men she was doing business with. She wanted an order from them.'

'And you agreed?'

Letitia nodded. 'Matthew begged me to do it to protect his career as well as mine.'

'I see. Is that all?'

Letitia hesitated. For a moment she wondered if she had said enough. But if she wanted to get his sympathy she had to tell him the rest of it. 'She wanted me to go to bed with her too.'

She saw the corners of his eyes narrow and he gave a little cough.

'Oh dear, that is very serious.'

'Matthew was there too. I got the feeling . . . That's why I came to see you, I suppose. I got the feeling that they were in on it together, that they had set me up.'

'That isn't very nice, is it?'

'No.'

'Had you ever . . . I mean, had you had an experience with a woman before?' Letitia thought she detected a slight quickening of his speech as he asked the question.

'No. Never. I didn't know what else to do. Now she's got something else planned. The only thing I could think of doing was to come and see you. I couldn't go on like this. I know I'm going to lose my job but I don't see why they should get away with it.'

'Quite so, quite so. But you say you're not sure whether Matthew was actually involved or, like you, just a victim of his wife's machinations?'

'No.'

'And what do you expect me to do?'

'I don't know. I just wanted you to hear it from me and not from Ursula. I just wanted to explain the situation. I know you are dead against adultery and I

120

suppose I am too, but I wanted you to hear my side too.'

'Mmm . . .' Piers sank back in the big leather seat, leaning his head on the headrest. After a moment he turned to her again. 'My dear, I wonder if I could ask you to do something for me?'

'Of course.'

'Would you have dinner with me tonight? I live alone, as you probably know, since my wife died a year ago. I would welcome a little company. My house-keeper is a really excellent cook and she always makes enough for two.'

Letitia was astonished by this request. She had expected moral outrage and a long diatribe against modern values. She had definitely not expected Piers' rather cool and sympathetic tone, nor an invitation to dinner. He seemed to have taken her news with surprising equanimity. It might just be that her play for his sympathy had worked.

'Thank you, I'd like that.' And it was true. She was not accepting the invitation merely because it was expedient. She found she had a real affinity with the man.

'Good. We're almost there. Let's have another glass of whisky.'

Piers Green lived in a flat-fronted Georgian town house in the centre of Mayfair. It had once been two houses that he had had knocked together, he explained to her, as he led her into the entrance hall, tiled in chequered black and white marble tiles.

The sitting room was spacious and comfortable, with large sofas grouped around an impressive fireplace, the walls painted white to show off a collection of oil paint-ings. Letitia recognised, with astonishment, a small Degas and a large Paul Klee. There were several equally striking paintings by artists she did not know.

'This is beautiful,' she said, looking at the Klee.

'I'm a rather eclectic collector,' he said.

At the back of the room, French windows opened on to a small but neatly planted garden. On a small terrace, surrounded by a trellis that dripped with honeysuckle, there was a cast-iron garden seat and a circular table. The white linen cloth on the table had been laid for one, solid silver cutlery, crystal glasses and a silver candelabra all brightly polished.

After Piers had poured Letitia another glass of whisky he went off to find his housekeeper. Moments later a chubby woman in a black dress appeared on the patio to set another place on the table.

The meal was delicious. They had cold asparagus and wild sea trout with tiny new potatoes and a salad. There was a chocolate cake, and *petits four* to go with demitasse cups of black coffee. The wine was a premier cru Chablis, followed, to go with the dessert, by a syrupy Sauternes. They talked about fashion, though not about lingerie, and about what Letitia had done prior to joining BSL. Piers seemed to be totally fascinated by everything she said.

As Letitia sipped her coffee she realised she had talked almost entirely about herself.

'So what about you?' she asked. 'Tell me about you.'

'When you get to my age, my dear, such a question could take the rest of my life to answer,' he said with a smile. 'I've been very lucky, let's leave it at that.'

Emboldened by the wine, as much as his attitude towards her, Letitia persisted. 'But what about this moral rearmament?'

He chuckled again. 'That has been rather overdone, if you must know. I was very happily married. I made a few statements to the press about that fact. The press being the press liked to make me out to be the defender of the faith when it came to marital values. They started talking about moral rearmament. I was never anything to do with that. Then recently I was on a television programme to discuss acquiring the Swedish paper mills we've just bought, and some daft reporter asked me if I thought Swedish morals when it came to sex would clash with my own views on the subject. I remarked that I thought men were too quick to forget their marriage vows. That much is true. I do believe that.'

'Matthew told me you had people fired for having affairs.'

'Nonsense. I had them fired because they weren't doing their jobs. But it wasn't a question of moral principle. I do think it is a bad idea for people working in the same company to become involved, especially if they're married. They spend so much time arranging secret assignations it gets in the way of their work. But that does not imply that I am setting myself up, or have ever set myself up, as a pillar of moral rectitude. Everything gets distorted.' He paused and took a sip of the desert wine. 'In fact,' he added, 'if I had met a girl as beautiful as you when I had been married I don't know what I would have done.'

'I take that as a compliment,' Letitia said. Piers was looking at her steadily, his eyes a very light blue.

'That's how it was intended.'

'The meal was wonderful.'

'Good.'

It had got dark over dinner but the terrace was lit by spotlights hidden among the foliage and providing a soft light. There was a single candle on the table which flickered in the slight breeze.

'I suppose I should think about getting home.'

'I wish you wouldn't.' He reached across the table and touched her hand, covering it with his. 'I can't tell you how much I have enjoyed this evening. It's so long since I just talked to anyone, someone who was uninvolved.'

'What do you mean?'

'Business tends to take over your life. Everything revolves around it, everyone you meet and talk to has some axe to grind.'

Letitia wasn't at all sure what to say. Piers seemed lonely and vulnerable and she felt a wave of sympathy for the man. She moved her other hand and laid it on top of his. 'I've enjoyed it too.'

'As for women . . . Do you have any idea what I have to put up with? I'm a wealthy man. A very wealthy man. If I go out to a do, women throw themselves at me, sometimes literally. All shapes and sizes. I have had more décolletage thrust under my nose than the photographers you use at BSL.'

'And do you ever accept?'

He shook his head. 'Never. I have never been convinced that they are interested in me as opposed to my money. Besides . . .' He stopped, staring down into his coffee cup.

'Besides what?' Letitia prompted, squeezing his hand.

'You are a very special woman, Letitia,' he said, suddenly very serious.

'Special, why?'

'Because I think I can tell you something I haven't ever been able to tell another woman other than my wife. Is that all right?'

'Of course.'

'I have . . . I can't . . .' He paused, then started again. 'When it comes to sex I have rather special needs.'

'I see,' Letitia said, trying to sound matter-of-fact. She wasn't at all sure why or how but a bond seemed to have developed between them. She genuinely liked him and felt sorry for him. 'I don't have to go home, Piers,' she found herself saying.

'Really?' She saw a glint of excitement spark in his eyes.

'If you don't want me to.'

'I would love you to stay.'

'Then why don't we go upstairs? We'd be more comfortable, wouldn't we, and we can continue our conversation.' Letitia felt remarkably calm considering what she was saying. Before she had met Matthew she would never have dared to be as bold but her experience with him had taught her to express her feelings much more frankly. She supposed that self-interest was playing its part; it would do no harm at all to have Piers on her side. But that was not her overriding motivation. Piers Green was an attractive man. Despite his age, power and wealth he had the air of a little boy lost in a world he found hard to understand, and for Letitia that was very appealing.

Piers was looking at her with those steely light-blue eyes. He got up and came around to the back of her chair, pulling it away as she got to her feet. Very gently he kissed her on the cheek. 'You are a very special woman.'

'And you're a gentleman,' she said, and meant it.

He took her by the hand and led her up the long straight staircase to the first floor. At the top of the stairs was a pair of panelled doors. He opened one of them and ushered her inside. His bedroom was large and lavish, toned in creams and oatmeals with a big bed. Elaborate curtains with pelmets and tiebacks surrounded the two large rectangular windows, and there was a thick cream-coloured carpet.

'You are going to have to forgive me,' he said. 'It's been a long time.'

She turned and smiled at him. Recently sex had been almost brutish in its urgency, a headlong dash to satisfy unreasoning need. Whatever Piers wanted, it was not going to be that, she was sure. It would make a pleasant change.

'Just tell me what you want, Piers.' She stroked his cheek and kissed him lightly on the mouth. She half expected him to draw her closer and kiss her more passionately, but he did not.

He went over to the curtains and drew them across the windows. The room was lit by two big china lamps sitting on bow-fronted mahogany chests on either side of the bed. He operated a small switch on one of them which dimmed them both, reducing the light to a pleasant glow.

'You really want me to tell you?'

'It's all right. Whatever it is, there's nothing to be ashamed of.' After what had happened with Ursula, she could state that as a fact.

'Will you take your dress off?' His voice was vibrato, almost a whisper.

'Unzip me then,' she said, turning her back on him. She heard the zip sing as he pulled it down.

Without a word Letitia turned around again and extracted her arms from the sleeves, then allowed the dress to fall away. Though she had not had the slightest idea she would be doing this, fortunately she was wearing a matching BSL bra and panties in black lace.

'Beautiful,' Piers muttered, apparently transfixed by the sight.

'And now?' she said gently.

'Would you lie on the bed?' he said. 'Don't bother with the counterpane, just lie on top of it.'

Letitia did exactly that. The bed was soft and she sank down into it.

Piers walked over to the bedside chest. She noticed his hand was trembling slightly as he opened the top drawer of the chest. But he took nothing out of it. He walked back to the foot of the bed and sat in a wing chair with a button back upholstered in a tweedy cream material.

'This is a lovely comfortable bed,' Letitia said. She raised her head to look at him. He had his elbows on the arms of the chair with his fingertips pressed together in an attitude of prayer, the index fingers resting against his lips, his eyes gazing at her body.

She thought she knew what he wanted now. Sitting up, she reached behind her back and unclipped her bra. Piers' gentleness was appealing in a totally different way to Matthew's obvious sensuality. It did not create that instant, electrifying lust but it was, in its own way, deeply affecting. There was something about the way he was looking at her, a hint of need, that made the familiar knot of excitement tighten in the pit of her stomach. She had never imagined that this would be the result of engineering her 'chance' meeting with Piers, but the improbability of it only added to the thrill.

She shucked herself out of her bra, her breasts tingling as she saw his eyes swivelling down to them, then lay back again, hooking her fingers into the waist-band of the tights. If she had known this was going to happen she would have worn black stockings. She kicked her shoes off then raised her bottom and pulled the tights down over her hips and stripped them away.

Very slowly and deliberately she ran her left hand up and down her throat, stroking it with the tips of her fingers, her forearm crushed against her breast. Then she gradually worked it down her collarbone and over the swell of her right breast until she reached the nipple.

She heard a soft moan and looked up at Piers. He was

127

staring at her, motionless, as though he had turned to stone.

Her nipples were only just beginning to stiffen. She pinched them both in turn to accelerate the process and felt a fierce twinge of pleasure. Gradually she allowed her hand to drop to her belly, lazily caressing her soft flesh.

She worked her hand down over the front of the panties and between her legs, feeling the pulpy folds of her labia under the material.

'You're very beautiful,' he said.

'Thank you.'

She saw that his right hand had moved to his lap and was rubbing the front of his trousers.

'Wouldn't you like to get more comfortable?' she asked.

'I will in a minute.'

'You want me to look in the drawer? Is that it?'

He nodded. 'If you wouldn't mind.'

Letitia rolled on to her side and stretched over to the bedside chest. She opened the drawer a little further and peered inside. The drawer was empty but for a black scarf, a small bottle of perfume and a long thin rectangular box. She took the items out. The box was bright yellow and wrapped in cellophane. What significance they had for Piers she did not know, but it was obviously considerable.

'Do you want me to open this?'

He nodded.

She tore the cellophane away and opened the lid of the box. It contained a cream torpedo-shaped plastic vibrator.

Letitia had never used a vibrator before and she wasn't at all sure what he wanted her to do with the black scarf. But she opened the perfume and sniffed it. It was a heavy, rather old-fashioned flowery scent.

'Mmm . . . I like it,' she said, though she wasn't sure she did. She took the stopper of the bottle and dabbed the perfume between her breasts and behind her ears.

'Oh, that is delightful on you,' he said, inhaling deeply.

'This is so soft,' she said, putting the bottle on the bedside chest and picking up the scarf. She flapped it out. The silk was of the finest quality, with a nap that reminded her of the bloom on a peach.

'Yes,' he said. 'So soft against the skin.'

That seemed to be a clue as to what he wanted. Letitia trailed the scarf across her body. The coolness and softness of it made her flesh pimple. 'It's lovely.'

'That's perfect,' he said.

'Like this.' She held the scarf up and allowed it to float down on to her chest. It was big enough to cover most of her torso. She left it there, her breasts and hard nipples outlined under the silk, and picked up the vibrator. There was a gnarled knob at the base of the phallus which she turned. Immediately a humming noise filled the air and she felt a remarkably strong vibration affecting her hand.

She touched the tip of the vibrator tentatively against her nipple. It pulsed strongly. Slowly she ran the point down over the black silk to her belly. As it touched the top of her panties the tendrils of vibrations reached her sex and she felt a pleasant tingle of pleasure. Moving the dildo down further made the tingling get stronger. It was not like any feeling she had experienced before, the vibrations seizing her clitoris and making it oscillate too, but the results were all too familiar. Deep in her sex she felt her nerves beginning to knot, the first precursor of orgasm.

Gently she eased the vibrator down over her sex, using the whole shaft now, pressing the smooth plastic cylinder into the channel between her labia. The strength of the vibrations increased dramatically. Her clitoris began to throb, sharp needles of sensation that set all her nerves on edge. The knot tightened.

Quickly she pulled the gusset of the panties to one side, and thrust the tip of the dildo down to the mouth of her vagina, wanting to feel the effect it would have there. Immediately the vibrations spread out through this new area of her labia, creating all sorts of fresh sensations. She pushed it up into her vagina and the sound of the humming lowered in pitch as the cream plastic slid inside. The feelings were delicious. Without thinking, obeying the dictates of her body now, she plunged the dildo up as far as it would go, until it disappeared almost entirely. She moaned. Suddenly the vibrations seemed to shimmer through every part of her sex, in her clitoris, at the neck of her womb and all around her labia. She had never felt anything like this. The vibrations were taking her over. It seemed every muscle and nerve in her body was vibrating, her breasts and nipples, her arms and legs, and each one of them produced the most wonderful trills and tremors of sensation. She scissored her legs together, trapping the dildo in the depths of her sex, and this created a whole new level of feeling, the gnarled butt of the dildo, which was vibrating as strongly as the rest of it, now trapped tightly between her labia and making them oscillate even more powerfully. This feeling was immediately transmitted to her clit, attacked now, or so it seemed, from two directions, from the dildo inside, radiating vibrations outward, and from the much more direct feelings travelling through her labia.

'Oh God . . .' Letitia cried. She had forgotten Piers. The dildo had directed everything inward. The more pressure she put on it the more the vibrations affected her. She felt her sex clenching around the hard, unyielding object that filled it, and receiving a huge kick of sensation in return. She was coming now, her orgasm breaking over the tip of the dildo, then rushing out in all directions, smothering her in pleasure, the unremitting vibration only seeming to deepen and extend every sensuous delight.

Eventually, and with a certain amount of reluctance, she opened her legs and turned the knob at the end of the dildo, allowing it to slide out of her body of its own accord. When it did, she shuddered. She was astonished at the effect the little machine had had on her. She had never thought to experiment with such things. It was another example of her lack of curiosity when it came to sex. She was a late developer but she intended to make up for lost time. Tomorrow she'd walk down to Soho in her lunch break and find a shop where she could buy one.

She raised her head and looked at Piers. He hadn't moved. His hand still frosted the front of his trousers.

Letitia felt selfish. She had been so overcome by what the vibrator was doing to her, she had entirely ignored his needs. 'Would you like me to do that for you?' she said.

'No, just . . . just hand me the scarf.' Letitia pulled the scarf from her body and got to her feet. She was aware of the strange scent that she had put on. It was clinging to the black silk. 'I'll do whatever you want, Piers, anything,' she said sincerely.

'I know, I know,' he said, his face looking anguished. He held out his hand and she handed him the scarf. Immediately he brought it up to his face, rubbing the silk against his mouth and nose.

'Let me,' she said.

She stood alongside the chair and took the scarf

again, covering his entire face with it, the thin material sucked in around his nose as he breathed deeply.

'Oh yes, like that,' he said.

His hand rubbed the front of his trousers aggressively. Suddenly his whole body went rigid and he gave out a little mewling sound, high-pitched and short. Then all the tension went out of him and he slumped back into the chair. 'Wonderful,' he said. 'My dear, you are quite wonderful.'

'More coffee?'

'No, I'd rather get home.'

'So soon.' He looked disappointed.

'Your home.'

'Oh.' An expression of almost schoolboy delight spread over Piers' face. That was what she liked about him. Even though over the last two days he had spoken to her every evening and sent her two bouquets of long-stemmed velvety crimson roses, each with a hand-written card telling her that he could not stop thinking about her, he had not assumed that their dinner date would end in bed. 'I'd like that too.'

'What are we waiting for then?' She finished the cognac she had ordered after what was probably one of the best meals she'd ever had in her life. La Poulette was a three-star Michelin restaurant with prices to match. They had both ordered the same thing, *mousseline de homard* followed by *canard challan*. Both were out of this world. The dessert had been a pistachio soufflé served with vanilla ice cream on the side and followed by a mountainous plate of *petits fours*. Piers had ordered a bottle of claret that was almost the same colour as the roses he'd sent her and tasted of blackcurrants and the scents of autumn. The brandy, a twenty-five-year-old

Delmain, was equally exceptional, and also a reminder of autumn, its colour the deep hue of equinoctial beech leaves.

Piers made the international sign for the bill, raising his hand and miming writing on it, and in seconds a waiter arrived with a folded piece of paper on a small white plate, the service, Letitia suspected, conditioned by the fact that Piers Green was obviously a regular and extravagant customer. He signed the paper without looking at it then got up, two waiters materialising to pull their chairs back.

The Silver Wraith was waiting at the front entrance, the chauffeur standing with the passenger door open, just as he had been three hours earlier when Piers had called to pick her up from her flat.

They climbed into the back.

'Straight home, sir?' the chauffeur asked.

'Yes, Fred, straight home.'

'Thank you, sir.'

This time it was the chauffeur who operated the switch that wound up the glass partition between driver and passengers.

'That was a wonderful meal,' Letitia said.

'And you are wonderful company, my dear. You look wonderful too.'

Letitia hoped so. She had spent nearly all her savings on the outfit, a beautifully cut but plain black cocktail dress with no sleeves, and a V-neck lined in black chiffon, its bodice tight and clinging while its skirt was flared. She'd bought new shoes too, black suede high heels, the heels coated in chrome.

'Thank you,' she said. 'I feel very comfortable with you, considering . . .'

'The age difference.'

'No, actually, I was going to say considering that you

133

run a multimillion-pound conglomerate and I work as a junior assistant in a design studio.'

'Put that way, I suppose you're right, it is extraordinary.'

'Can I ask you something?'

'Of course.'

'What are you going to do about the Silverstones?'

'I think I should double Matthew's bonus.'

'What!'

'I'm joking. But he was responsible for our meeting. I gather you haven't had any further trouble.'

'I was supposed to go there tonight. Ursula was having a little party.'

'Really. What did you say?'

'Nothing. I expect she's going to be very cross when I don't turn up.'

Don't worry, Letitia. You'll never be bothered by either of them again, I can promise you that.'

'I really like my job, Piers,' she said.

'What's Joy Skinner like?'

She was surprised he'd even heard of Joy Skinner. He had at least nine major companies under his control, with over six thousand employees. 'The best. I haven't been there long enough to really be sure, but she seems to make all the decisions where design and marketing are concerned. And everyone likes and respects her.'

'That's what I thought.'

The restaurant was only a mile away from Piers' Mayfair house and the car was soon pulling up outside.

Piers dismissed the chauffeur and led Letitia inside. The house was in darkness. He switched on the lights and turned off the burglar alarm.

'I gave my housekeeper the night off,' he explained.

'So we're all alone.' She stepped up to him and kissed

him lightly on the lips. She knew instinctively that he did not want any firmer contact.

'Letitia, after last time, well, I thought . . . I mean, you were so understanding. It's always been difficult for me. Sex, I mean. Since my wife died . . . she understood me so well, understood my . . .'

'Special needs.'

'Exactly. She knew exactly what I wanted, what I liked. I feel I can trust you in the same way.'

'You can.'

'It's been a long time since I've been able to . . . express myself . . .'

'I'll do whatever you want, Piers. You mustn't be afraid.' She meant it. It wasn't pity. She really liked the man. Yesterday, in her lunch break, she had gone to the library. She was curious to see what Piers' wife had looked like. There were pictures of Mr and Mrs Piers Green in the back copies of the *Times*. To Letitia's surprise Mrs Sharon Green had been considerably younger than her husband, a strawberry blonde who, on the evidence of pictures, liked to dress in a way that flaunted her considerable bust and rather meaty thighs. Seeing her lying on that big double bed drenched in perfume and performing for her husband with the black silk scarf and a powerful vibrator was not much of a feat of imagination. Letitia had wondered who had instigated the ritual, whether it was her idea or something Piers had thought up for himself.

'I thought . . .' he said hesitantly. 'I hoped you might come back with me, so I . . .'

'What? It's all right, you can say it.'

'Why don't you go up first. I left some things on the bed.'

'What sort of things?'

He blushed, his rather white face turning bright red. 'Lingerie.'

'Mmm . . . that sounds like fun. Why don't you give me ten minutes to get ready?'

'Yes.'

She kissed him on the cheek and climbed the stairs. She wasn't at all sure how she felt about her relationship with Piers. It had certainly solved all her problems as far as the Silverstones were concerned. In fact, she was hoping Ursula would phone her in a rage so she could have the pleasure of telling her that she had not been able to attend her soirée as she had been out to dinner with Piers Green. That would definitely take the wind out of her sails. And she certainly had no objection to the extravagant dinners and the chauffeur-driven Rolls Royce. But she had the feeling that though she was comfortable and relaxed in his company there was a side to Piers she had not seen yet. She knew his reputation for ruthless business dealings and found it hard to reconcile this with the almost diffident face he presented her with. It was probably jumping the gun to begin to think in terms of a long-term relationship, but she would also find it impossible to have feelings for a man who was so inhibited when it came to physical contact. Piers Green was not a man who liked to kiss or cuddle.

She opened the bedroom door. The curtains had been drawn, the lights dimmed and the bedding drawn back. Lying on the white linen sheet was a white satin basque, the cups of its bra made from delicate lace. Next to it was a pair of white high-heeled shoes, and white stockings with broad lacy white welts. The top drawer of the bedside chest was open and inside she saw the same items, except that the black silk scarf had been replaced with a white one.

Letitia needed to pee. She went into the en suite bathroom and used the toilet, then took off her dress. She had chosen her lingerie as carefully as her dress, more samples of BSL design, but they were clearly not required and she stripped them off and hung them over the side of the bath. Naked, Letitia walked back into the bedroom. She picked up the basque and wrapped it around her waist, the satin cool to the touch. She hooked it up on the tightest of the three positions provided at the back, then sat on the bed to roll on the stockings. This little ritual had become so much a part of her preparations for sex recently that watching the white nylon rolling out over her leg gave her a little trill of excitement. With the stockings clipped into the suspenders of the basque, she levered her feet into the shoes. Letitia took out the three items from the drawer. She wondered how many other women had been asked to perform for him in this way. As he appeared so shy and retiring, perhaps he had hired prostitutes to satisfy his exact requirements. Not that it mattered. What he wanted from her was undoubtedly bizarre but, after what had happened with Ursula, she found she could cope with it without compunction. At least she was here of her own free will. There was no element of threat hanging over her head.

She applied the perfume – Sharon Green's perfume she was sure – to her breasts, her neck and the tops of her thighs, then lay back on the bed. She opened her legs and bent them at the knee, digging the heels into the sheet. Experimentally she caressed her labia. She was not surprised to find they were already moist.

If she had tried to imagine something completely opposite to what she had experienced with Matthew and with Ursula, this was it. With them she had been swept along on a tidal wave of passion, unable to control her reactions. With Piers, on the other hand, there was an almost clinical detachment. But though the experience was different it was no less exciting; just as the element of the forbidden had excited her with the Silverstones, this ritual aroused her for the same reasons.

She remembered how she had masturbated for Tom. She had never quite worked out what had possessed her to do it. She had thought about it a lot. It was probably that she had reached a point in her life when she was ready to experiment, bored with the sexual rut she had allowed herself to become stuck in and looking for a excuse to experiment. The way Matthew had looked at her at her interview and what he had made her feel – though she still did not understand how – in combination with the effect of wearing the sensuous black stockings for the first time had been the excuse she needed to put her own needs first. She had opened her mind and her body to new experiences. Everything had followed from that. Without it she would never have been ready for Matthew and would never have reacted with such wild passion.

And that was what she was feeling now. Even though she was acting out Piers, sexual fantasy, she was in control. In recent weeks she had learnt to use sex, not just be possessed by it. In the past, sex had been something that was done to her. She would never have been able to participate in what Piers was asking her to do, this ritual performance imitating, she was sure, what Sharon Green had done. But now she had the confidence to explore the more outré and not be intimidated by it, and that confidence was exhilarating. She hadn't forgotten the effects of the vibrator either. She had been astonished at how it had made her feel, how the vibrations had seemed to reach right into the core of her. That was definitely something she was eager to experience again.

Taking hold of the dildo, she brought it up to her mouth and licked it obscenely, imagining for a moment that it was Matthew's cock. Despite all her doubts as to his role in his wife's plans, she still felt her heart thump with desire when she thought of the things they had done together. With the tip covered in her saliva she pushed the dildo into the slit of her sex. It nudged against her clitoris, which pulsed instantly. As she nosed it into her vagina it slid home easily and she gasped as the hard plastic parted her wet, pulpy flesh and rode right up to the neck of her womb.

She looked down at her body, the dildo wedged firmly between her legs, her thighs banded by the tight lacy white stocking tops, the suspenders stretching the nylon taut. Sex with Matthew and the others had been spontaneous and urgent, a headlong rush of raw passion. This was calculated and deliberate, even cerebral, but she could still feel her pulse racing and her breath beginning to shorten.

'Are you ready for me?' Piers said from outside the door.

'See for yourself.'

Piers shuffled into the room. He was wearing a silk paisley robe and velvet slippers, his legs bare.

'I started without you,' Letitia said, undulating her hips. She allowed the vibrator to slip down until only the tip was still hidden in the lips of her sex. 'This makes me feel so sexy, Piers.'

'You look wonderful.'

'Thank you.'

He sat in the wing chair and crossed his legs. They were covered with thick blond hairs.

'Do you want to touch?' she asked, hoping to encourage him to be a little more interactive.

He shook his head. His eyes were roaming her body,

taking in every detail of the white lingerie and the way it clung to her. She wondered if he were imagining his wife lying there.

Letitia thrust the vibrator back up into her body and moaned softly. She could feel the sticky juices of her sex coating the cream plastic.

'Tell me about Ursula,' Piers said in a perfectly calm and level voice.

'What do you want to know?' The request surprised Letitia, but she didn't betray that in her tone. She had thought about Ursula a lot over the last week, going over in her mind everything she had done to her. As much as she would have liked to convince herself that the experience had been less than exhilarating, the truth was that if the woman had asked to do it all over again, she wasn't at all sure what she'd say. She wondered if Ursula used a dildo. Would that have been the next stage in her sexual education? The thought of Ursula's artful tongue licking her clitoris while she held the powerfully vibrating dildo deep inside her sex made a flutter of delectation run through her.

'I like to watch, Letitia, watch and listen.'

This was a new piece in the sexual jigsaw, but Letitia willingly picked up her cue.

'Ursula is a very beautiful woman.'

'Yes. Very beautiful. What did she make you do?'

Letitia moved the dildo in and out of her vagina gently. She felt her clitoris pulsing, as if trying to draw attention to itself. She eased the middle finger of her free hand down into her labia and covered her clit. 'I'd never been to bed with a woman before.'

'You'd never kissed a woman before? What was it like?'

'Different. Softer.'

'But exciting?'

140

'Yes. It made me wet.' The last word made him whimper.

'What sort of breasts did she have?'

'Big. Fleshy. They drooped slightly under their own weight. Small nipples.'

'Did you hold them?'

Letitia had a strange feeling that all these questions had been asked before, just like the masturbation ritual. Had his wife been bisexual? she wondered.

'Yes, and kiss them.'

'Soft and fleshy,' he whispered. She saw his hand was rubbing against the front of his robe. 'Did that excite you?'

'I didn't think it would at first. But it did. When I kissed her our breasts squashed together. That was really exciting. My nipples were so hard they were like little stones, but so were hers. I could feel them.' Letitia felt her sex contracting strongly as she drove the dildo into it.

'And did she touch you, down there, I mean?' He nodded to the apex of her thighs.

'Oh yes. And kissed it too.'

'Together? Did you do it together?'

'Not at first. First she did all the work. She was so good at it. She kissed me down here.' Letitia angled her sex up towards him. 'She was so good at it, she made me come.'

'That was the first time a woman had done that to you?'

'I'd never felt anything like it. Never. She was kissing my pussy then she swung herself up over me.'

'Sitting on top of you?'

'Yes. I could see her, Piers. Everything. And I knew what she wanted me to do.'

Letitia switched the dildo on and crammed it into her

141

body. This running commentary was exciting her quite as much as it was Piers. She could see Ursula's body in her mind's eye and remember the feeling as she had raised her mouth to the other woman's smooth, hairless sex. The vibrations radiated outward, raising her sexual temperature immediately, the beginnings of orgasm teasing her nerves.

'I wrapped my hands around her thighs and levered myself up. It was the first time I'd done anything like that. I ran my tongue into her labia. They were so silky and so wet.' She began rolling her finger over her clit, her sex clenched tightly around the plastic phallus quite as hard as any fist. The more strongly she gripped it the more potent the vibrations seemed to be and the more they affected her. The waves of pleasure that coursed through her were making it difficult for her to talk but she persisted, the mental image she was conjuring up amplifying her excitement. 'Then she was doing it to me again.' She remembered that moment more graphically than any other, the shock of pure pleasure as Ursula's mouth had settled on her sex for a second time. She pulled the dildo down the long sleek tube of her sex then thrust it back up again, the vibrations affecting every nerve, her clitoris spasming against her finger. She arched off the bed, felt her eyes forced closed by an intense sensation at the back of her eyeballs, and came, her body trembling helplessly on the big bed.

When she opened her eyes Piers was slumped in the chair, his body inert, a wet stain spreading over the front of the silk robe.

'You're a remarkable woman, Letitia,' he said as she sat up, pulling the dildo from her sex.

'You're a remarkable man, Piers,' she replied. And that was certainly true.

142

Chapter Six

'*DO YOU LIKE IT?*'

'Of course.' Letitia glanced around the office. It was on the first floor, with a large picture window, white walls and a dark-grey carpet. There was a large drawing board with a pedestal unit full of sketching pens and inks and all the material needed to draw.

'Good. I've spoken to Daniel. He wants you to work out a complete new range.' Joy Skinner was smiling.

'Just on the basis of my sketches?'

'Yes. He's very impressed. And so am I. You've got two weeks.'

'I've done a lot of work already.' Last week Letitia had delivered three new designs to Daniel Travis for a bra, a pair of panties and a camisole, all matching the same basic design tenets she had used on the teddy. 'But what about you? I'm supposed to be your assistant.'

Joy grinned. 'There's going to be a reorganisation around here, Letitia. I can't tell you much yet because it's still all hush-hush. But I'll be getting a more administration-orientated assistant, if you know what I mean.'

'Is it promotion for you?'

'I can't say anything else,' Joy said, but from the look on her face it was a move she clearly relished. 'There's going to be an announcement next week.'

'That's great.'

'Of course, you get a salary increase to go with the office. Accounts will give you all the details.'

'Really?'

'So you'd better get started. We need a full slip, a half slip, bikini panties, thong-cut panties, French knickers, a suspender belt, a soft-cup bra, an underwired bra, and two basques, one full length with a three-quarter-cup bra, and the other much more risqué, use your imagination as long as it's sexy. We're going to use the new Lycra-based material, but there's also that stretch velveteen option too, so you'll need to work out at least six colourways. If you've got time, look at a body too, again something risqué. High-cut legs, low-cut front, something for seduction, not wearing to work.'

Letitia had grabbed a pen and scribbled it all down on the paper lying on the drawing board.

'There's no problem about stuff for the catalogue, we've got months to look at that, but I'm thinking of putting out a new range for the retail business. I want to look at your stuff with that in mind, so the sooner the better.'

'I thought the new retail range wasn't due until next year.'

Joy Skinner tapped the end of her small rounded nose. 'Watch this space,' she said.

'I'll get right to work then.'

'Do that.'

Joy spun on her heel and walked out.

Letitia sat at the stool positioned in front of the drawing board. She wanted to call Piers and tell him the good news, even though she half suspected it was something to do with him. But he was in New York, and though he had called her last night, in fact every night since he'd left a week ago, and she had his number, the time difference made it impossible to call him so early.

Though outwardly everything had appeared unchanged at Black Stockings Lingerie company, Letitia suspected a lot had been going on behind the scenes. There had been closed doors and private meetings and wild rumours among the staff. Joy's announcement this morning was the first official hint that things were going to change, and Letitia suspected Piers Green had more than a little to do with it.

She was sure it was for the same reason that the call she had expected from Ursula Silverstone, after she'd failed to turn up at her party, had never materialised, as much as she'd hoped it would. Piers Green had clearly spoken to the Silverstones, either collectively or individually. What he had said or what he intended to do still remained a mystery, but Letitia had seen no sign of Ursula since, and very little of Matthew, who had kept himself very much to himself.

She guessed that Piers had called in Joy Skinner and was reorganising the whole company. She didn't care that much either. Not only had she got the Silverstones off her back, she had been given the sort of opportunity she had always dreamt about. And, though she was sure Piers had put in a good word for her, Daniel had made enough encouraging noises about her first design to make her believe her promotion wasn't entirely down to Piers' influence. She knew she had talent and now she had a chance to prove it.

She needed to work hard. She had already done a lot of sketches of some of the items Joy had mentioned, but getting them drawn up and coloured in a form good enough to impress Daniel was going to take a lot of time. There were also the new items Joy wanted, like the two basques and the French knickers, which she would need to start from scratch. She picked up a pen and began to sketch out the figure of a woman on the large drawing board.

It was well after six when she finally decided to call it a day. She went down to the studio to say goodnight to Joy but it, like the rest of the office, was deserted. Walking out on to the street she headed towards the tube.

'Letitia,' The voice came from behind her. She turned around. Ursula Silverstone was leaning out of the window of her grey Mercedes 500SL. 'Can I give you a lift?'

Ursula looked stunning. She was wearing a tight white wrap-over blouse and a short black leather skirt with a split on her left thigh, her soft wavy auburn hair catching the late-afternoon sun. 'No,' Letitia said curtly, striding away.

She heard the car's engine surge up behind her. 'I need to talk to you, Letitia, please. I know what I did was wrong. But don't tell me you didn't enjoy it. I know you did. Please just let me drive you home.'

Letitia stopped. Why not? she thought. She had nothing to fear from Ursula any more. Oddly, perhaps, considering what had happened between them, she felt no anger towards the woman. Besides, it was a hundred times better than riding home on the tube. 'All right,' she said.

Ursula leant over and opened the passenger door as Letitia walked around the car. She jumped in and Ursula gunned the engine, the short skirt revealing the muscles of her thighs as they worked the pedals. She was wearing glossy black tights.

Letitia stared at her legs and, to her surprise, felt a sudden surge of lust. Annoyed with herself at this reaction, she asked testily, 'So what is all this about?'

'I need your help. *We* need your help.'

'How come?'

'Hasn't Piers told you?'

Clearly Ursula knew of her relationship with Piers. But that was not a surprise.

'He's in New York.'

'You went to him, didn't you? Told him what had happened.'

'Yes.'

'I don't blame you. It was my fault. I was an idiot. Piers is asking Matthew to stand down as managing director. He wants Joy Skinner to take over. That's not a problem in itself. Piers was grooming Matt for another job in the group, a much bigger job. It's something he really wanted, a terrific opportunity . . .'

'So what do you want me to do?'

'Couldn't you explain? Couldn't you tell him you made a mistake? I mean, that you misinterpreted what happened?'

'Why should I do that?'

'Because I'm asking you to, begging you to.'

'I don't think he'd believe me. Ursula.'

'Couldn't you try? If Matthew loses his job at BSL and doesn't get Piers to give him another chance at the new company, he'll be finished.'

The car was heading into Regent's Park. People lay on the grass, taking in the sun. Letitia glanced at Ursula. She was wearing a white satin bra, her big breasts spilling over the top of it, the blouse veiling the ballooning flesh. Letitia felt another pulse of desire. It was the first time she had ever experienced that with a woman.

'Will you tell me the truth?'

'Of course.'

'Was Matthew in on it? Did he tell you he was taking me to the company flat that night?'

'No, of course not.'

'Why did you turn up then?'

'You know what Matthew's like. He's an attractive man. He's had lots of affairs. He knows that I like women. If you want to know the truth, we had come to a sort of accommodation. I arranged a little threesome with a friend of mine who was also bisexual. We used to get together every so often, no holds barred. I thought it would stop Matt playing around. But it didn't. I could see all the signs: staying out late, pretending he was working, not wanting sex when he got home. Well, I wasn't going to put up with it again. I was sick of it. I knew he used the company flat, so when he told me he wasn't going to be home until late that night I was sure I'd catch him there. And I did.'

'So shouldn't you be delighted that he's got his come-uppance?'

'I'd never have gone to Piers. I was bluffing. That would have been cutting off my nose to spite my face. I just wanted to make him suffer.'

'And me.'

'Yes, and you.'

'Is that the truth?' Letitia wasn't sure whether to believe her. She would clearly say anything to save Matthew's job.

'Yes.'

'And what about the last time, in the hotel?'

'I wanted him there. I thought that if I could persuade you to get involved in a threesome we could go back to what we had before. It was all my idea. Not Matthew's.'

'But you told him about it.'

'Yes.'

'And he agreed?'

'What choice did he have?'

Letitia thought about that as the Mercedes manoeu-

148

vred in the heavy traffic around Camden Town. It had the ring of truth. 'So you're telling me that was the only time he knew what you had planned?'

'Yes, of course. He kept begging me not to involve you.'

Letitia stared out at the traffic.

'Well, will you help?'

Letitia had learnt one lesson from Ursula. You don't get something for nothing.

'You're in the retail trade, right?'

'Yes.'

'Do you know Gordon Prentiss?'

'Yes.'

'I'll try and help you if you get me an introduction to him.'

'All right. But why? He gets all his lingerie from Mirage. He takes their whole line. He's not going to do a deal with BSL.'

'Just get me an introduction.'

Gordon Prentiss was the head of the biggest clothing retail group in Europe, with stores in five EC countries, and the largest turnover in the whole community. At her last job, his company had been their biggest customer and she had got to know one of their buyers. Letitia had already mentioned the contact to Joy Skinner but she was convinced they would never leave Mirage. If Letitia could get to Gordon Prentiss personally, she thought she might be able to change his mind. That would not only enhance Joy's position, but her own, especially if the deal was partly do to with her new designs. There was no harm in thinking big.

'All right. I think he's coming to the do at the Connaught next week. The Cancer Research benefit thing. I'll get you a ticket.'

'I'll be there.'

'How are you?'

'I'm very happy, Piers. But you know that, don't you?'

'About what?'

'About my promotion.'

'Promotion? No. I promoted Joy. It'll be announced next week. Matthew is stepping down. It was Joy's decision to promote you.'

'She didn't consult you?'

'No. And she doesn't know anything about you and me, in case you think she was trying to curry favour. You must have got the job on your own merits.'

Letitia liked to think he was telling the truth.

'Listen, I can't get back until Saturday.'

'That's all right.'

'Could we have dinner?'

'As long as we don't go out to a restaurant. I want to spend some time alone with you. It'll be over ten days.'

'Actually, that's why I was calling.'

It was eleven thirty and Letitia had just got into bed when the phone rang. 'Go on.'

'I've been thinking so much about you, Letitia.'

'Good. I've been thinking about you too.'

'I really . . . what you did . . .'

'Can I ask you something, Piers?' She might not have asked him face to face, but the telephone and the distance made it easier.

'Of course.'

'Have you ever . . . has anyone else done those things for you?'

He laughed. 'No, never. That's what made you so special. I told you women were always throwing themselves at me. I supposed it would have been easy enough to ask one of them. But I needed to feel it wasn't just something they were doing to please me, that they weren't faking it.'

'I understand.'

'I trust you now, Letitia. That's why I can ask you this.' Obviously the phone made things easier for him too.

'Go on.'

'What you were telling me about Ursula. You and Ursula.'

'Yes?'

'I found that very exciting. Very. You were excited too, weren't you? I mean, by the things she did to you?'

'Yes.'

'That's what I thought. I wondered if you'd like to do it again. With another woman, not Ursula of course, that would be too embarrassing. I just wondered if you'd like to experiment again, that's what it was, wasn't it, an experiment? Except this time I'd be there too.' It came out in a rush.

'You want to watch?'

'The real thing. Is that outrageous?'

It *was* outrageous, but the idea gave Letitia a sudden pulse of excitement, her exhibitionist fantasy clearly still running deep in her sexual psyche.

'I don't mind who it is. Don't answer me now. Just think about it. Will you do that?'

'Of course I will, Piers. Where are you now?' The shock of excitement had translated itself into a warm glow, radiating from between her sex. She spread her thighs apart under the single sheet.

'In my hotel suite.'

'Are you alone?'

'Yes.'

'Do you know where I am?'

151

Letitia felt her nipples stiffen. She tweaked her left one with her free hand. It responded with a fierce pulse of pleasure.

'No,' he said.

'I'm lying in bed, stretched out in bed.'

'Sounds lovely.'

'Do you know what I'm wearing?'

'Tell me.' His voice had become breathless.

'Very tight black satin panties. And black stockings. Hold-ups, you know the sort that don't need suspenders and cling to the thigh.' She threw the sheet to one side and looked at her body. 'I'm taking one of my breasts in my hand and squeezing it to a point. My nipples are stone hard. Oh, that feels good.'

'I bet it does.'

'I'm going to spread my legs apart. I've got a mirror in my room, opposite the bed. I can see the black satin covering my sex, Piers. It's tight. And dimpled, like my pussy's trying to suck it in. Can you imagine that?'

'Yes.'

'Hold on a minute. I've got to reach over to the bedside table.'

'What are you doing that for?'

'Because I went out and bought myself a vibrator. I've been practising with it.' Letitia wasn't lying about that. The cream plastic vibrator, identical to the one Piers had given her to use, was standing on its end on the bedside table. She'd bought it three days ago and had used it every night since, with devastating results.

'Have you?' His voice was so hoarse it was almost breaking up.

'I love it. There, that's better.' She ran the tip of the phallus down over her belly. 'I'm running it down my body. Over my belly. My clitoris is throbbing. Oh yes, I

152

haven't even touched it yet and I can feel it swelling. God, I'm so sensitive.'

'You are, I know. It's wonderful.'

'I'm going to have to wriggle out of these panties. Can you see me doing that, pulling them down over my thighs? Pulling them over the stockings?' She scissored her legs together and quickly tore off her panties. When she opened her legs again she could swear she could feel the mouth of her vagina opening. She was already wet and sticky.

'Oh yes.'

'That's better. Now I'm going to put it right up against my clit and turn it on. It always makes me come really quickly like that. If I put it inside, deep inside, it takes longer, doesn't it?'

'Yes.'

'Oh . . .' She pressed the phallus into her clit. It reacted with a huge wave of pleasure, throbbing hard against the cold plastic. She turned the gnarled knob at the end of the shaft and the vibrations shot through her. She had discovered with Piers that words could turn her on quite as much as actions, and her body was already primed. The vibrations were so powerful that for a moment she could not speak. 'Can you hear it?'

'Yes . . .' It was almost a whisper.

'Oh Piers, it's so good. I'm pressing it down harder. I'm going to put a finger in my pussy.' She nestled the phone into the pillow by her ear, freeing her right hand, then arched her buttocks off the bed and slid her hand under them. Her fingers found the open maw of her vagina and pushed inside, one at first, and then two. This produced another surge of sensation. Already she was on the brink of orgasm, but she managed to hold herself back. She wanted him to come first. 'There, two fingers, Piers. Can you imagine me doing that for you?

153

Letting you watch?' Letting him watch. The words made her whimper.

'Oh yes . . .' Suddenly there was an odd noise, half cough, half cry.

Letitia jammed the dildo hard against her clit, pushed her fingers deeper into the sticky tube of her sex and allowed the vibrations to take her over the brink, her orgasm swamping her, her body trembling under its impact. She made a long, low, keening noise that tailed off only when her orgasm had begun to relinquish its control.

'God, that was good,' she said, turning off the vibrator.

'You're a remarkable woman, Letitia.'

She was beginning to think it was true.

The restaurant at the Connaught was decked out in flowers and finery, the five-hundred-pound tickets ensuring that the guests were equally well dressed, the women in stunning *haute couture*, amazing creations of chiffon, lace, silk and satin. In contrast the men wore the customary uniform, evening suits with black ties, the only variation being the occasional white jacket among the serried ranks of black, and the different-coloured cummerbunds, bright scarlet, dark blue and even a primrose yellow. There was a sprinkling of celebrities, politicians, television personalities, actors and pop stars, the latter group the most flamboyantly dressed, a girl singer in a shiny black rubber jumpsuit that clung to every inch of her voluptuous figure, her huge platform-soled rubber boots adding inches to her height.

The room had been divided into round tables each holding twelve people, and Ursula had managed to wheedle herself and Letitia on to the same table as Gordon Prentiss.

Letitia had found a sheer bias-cut silk dress dusted with glass beads. It had a thigh-length skirt with a flounced hem and a draped neck, its tight waist clinging to the natural contours of her body. Naturally it was red, a dark rose red. She had persuaded the accounts department to give her an advance on her salary to pay for it.

Gordon Prentiss was young, considering his position as chairman and chief executive of the huge and rapidly expanding retail group he had built up. As the after-dinner speakers, an ageing fast bowler who had played cricket for England, and a once famous but now retired television presenter, indulged in none too amusing reminiscences of their respective lives, Letitia studied him across the table. The financial pages of the newspapers gave his age as thirty-seven, but he looked younger. He was very tall and on the thin side of slender, with a rather long face, a straight nose and a great shock of dark-brown wiry hair which appeared immune to any sort of grooming, other than a side parting. His companion was a raven-haired brunette with an olive complexion, black eyes and high sharp cheekbones, her loose-fitting white slip dress, its spaghetti straps encrusted with diamanté, making it perfectly obvious that her rather small breasts were not encumbered by a bra.

The speeches finally ended and waiters began to refill the coffee cups and brandy glasses that littered the tables. Cigars were lit and people got up and began to mill around the tables.

'Come on,' Ursula said. She nodded at Gordon Prentiss, who had just got to his feet. 'This is your chance.'

Ursula led Letitia around the table.

'Ursula,' Prentiss said. 'This is a pleasure.' He kissed her on both cheeks. Ursula was wearing a cowl-neck top in peachy silk with a long tight skirt to match. His eyes appraised her outfit critically, taking a professional interest in every detail.

'Gordon, how are you? Haven't seen you for ages.'

'We must have dinner. How's Matthew?'

'He's fine. I just wanted to introduce you to Letitia Drew, one of our bright new designers.'

Gordon turned to Letitia and held out his hand. She shook it. 'I'm delighted to meet you,' she said.

'Likewise. May I introduce Maria Alvarez de Veiga.'

'How do you do?' the brunette said in perfectly accented English. She shook hands with Ursula and Letitia in turn.

'Maria is setting up a new Spanish operation for me.'

'How interesting,' Ursula said. 'Have you been in retailing long?' Skilfully Ursula guided Maria to one side, leaving Letitia alone with Gordon.

'So you're a designer, are you?' he said.

'Yes. I'm working on a whole new range for BSL.' It felt strange to be called a designer at last, but after all, it was now perfectly true.

'They make some good stuff. Matthew's pitched to us a few times, but it's never been quite what we're looking for.'

'I'd really like to show you what I've done.'

Gordon looked at her steadily for a moment. 'Why don't you give my office a call and make an appointment?'

'Because if I do that I'll never see you again.'

Gordon laughed. 'You're right.'

'It's all right. I can take rejection. You only have to say you're not interested. You don't have to get someone else to do it for you.'

Gordon was still smiling. 'It's nice to meet someone who is so direct.' He took his wallet from his inside

156

pocket and extracted a white business card from it. 'Here. That's my home number and my mobile. I'm going away for a couple of days but I'm back on Friday. Give me a ring and we'll get together over the weekend.'

That was ideal for Letitia. She had worked on her designs all week and at least six items were being made up into samples. The extra time would give her a chance to see that they were all properly finished, and not merely tacked together.

'That's really very kind of you.'

'No, I look forward to it, I believe in rewarding initiative. And you've certainly shown that.'

'Thank you.'

'Now, if you'll excuse me I've got an early start in the morning.'

He turned to Maria, said goodbye to Ursula, and guided the Spanish woman across the room to the exit.

'Well, did you get what you wanted?' Ursula asked.

'I think so.' She held up the little white card. 'We'll have to see.'

'Do you want to stay?'

'Not really.'

'Good. These things are always so boring.'

Ursula had ordered a car to pick them up and take them to the Connaught, and it was waiting outside among the massed ranks of other such limousines. As they walked out of the porticoed entrance, their driver spotted them and immediately swung his car, a black Daimler Princess, around to the entrance. He jumped out and ran around to open the passenger door.

They climbed into the cavernous rear seat.

'Where to, madam?' the driver asked when he'd got back behind the wheel, winding down the glass partition between the front and rear seats.

'Kentish Town, then Highgate,' Ursula said.

'Certainly, madam,' he said. The glass partition whirred upward again.

'So I've kept my part of the bargain,' Ursula said. 'Will you keep yours?'

'I'll try. I could think of something that would make it easier.' Letitia had seen Piers twice since he had returned from America, and on both occasions had indulged in the ritual which was all he seemed to want when it came to sex. Again he had provided items of lingerie for Letitia to wear and again he had shied away from anything but the briefest physical contact. He did not mention directly the subject he had raised on the phone from New York but Letitia guessed he hoped it wouldn't be necessary. If she didn't care to indulge his wilder fantasies that was up to her. But if she did, she imagined he was waiting for her to surprise him.

She had thought long and hard about Piers. It was odd how easily she had fallen into a relationship with him and how quickly she had come to accept the bizarre sexual games he wanted to play. She had certainly never had a relationship with a man that was like this, but then she had never been out with a multimillionaire before. Piers was a man who was used to getting what he wanted. He had been slow to pluck up the courage to ask a woman to cater for his fantasies since the death of his wife, but now he had finally conquered his inhibitions, she was sure it wouldn't take him so long next time. That particular cat was out of the bag. If he wanted to take the ritualised voyeurism a stage further and she was not prepared to co-operate, she was sure it would not take him a year before he found another woman who was.

Not that she was concerned about that. After the first night together Piers had been so eager to see her again, and so insistent, that he hadn't given her the chance to ask herself if she really wanted to see him. Subsequently she had discovered that she did, that she genuinely liked the man and even, in the mood of sexual adventure that had happily coincided with their meeting, enjoyed the games he wanted to play in the bedroom. But she was not trying to reel Piers in like a fish on a line with the ultimate aim of marriage and concomitant wealth. In fact, that idea had never occurred to her. She thought of her relationship with Piers only in the short term.

She couldn't kid herself, however, that she was acting entirely out of friendship. Of course it was pleasant to eat at the best restaurants in town and be driven around in a Rolls-Royce. Nor could she pretend that his position in relation to BSL hadn't got her out of an awkward situation. Though she felt sure she could have succeeded on her own merits, she wasn't naive enough to believe either that her sudden promotion hadn't been, at least in part, down to him, despite his denials.

And she wasn't ready to give up the benefit of his power and influence just yet, especially if she wanted to help Matthew. She liked to think that if the suggestion he'd made on the phone had been sexually repugnant she would have walked away. But it wasn't. What had happened with Ursula had shocked her, it was true; it had also been profoundly arousing. Had she known Matthew was watching it would have been even more so. This time there would be no doubt everything she did would be closely observed, adding fuel to the bonfire of unaccustomed desires.

'Go on,' Ursula said, interrupting her train of thought.

'Well . . .' She hesitated. Like Piers, her inhibitions had disappeared. 'Piers wants to see me with another woman.'

'What!'

'He likes to watch, Ursula. That's his thing.'

'And he wants to watch you with a woman?'

'Yes.'

'My God, I bet that's what Sharon did,' Ursula said, thinking aloud.

'Really?'

'Sharon was a dyke. I mean, not bisexual, a real dyke. She even made a play for me once. Everyone always wondered how she managed to keep him. That must be what she did, arranged little shows for him with one of her girlfriends.'

'I think she used to do other things too.' For the first time in recent weeks Letitia felt herself blushing. 'She might even have got him hooked on the whole voyeuristic thing. He's not very feely. He doesn't like to touch.'

'You mean she used to let him watch her wank?' The word sounded strange in Ursula's cultured accent.

'Yes.'

'And that's what he wants you to do too?'

'Yes.'

'OK. Let's do it.'

'It's not as easy as that. He doesn't want you. He said it would be too embarrassing. I suppose because he knows you too well.'

'So you discussed me then?'

'I told him what happened between us, yes.'

'Well, that's a pity. And presumably as you're such a novice in such matters you don't have any dykey friends.'

'No. And anyway I don't know how I'd feel with someone else.'

Ursula pulled the car to a halt three or four doors down from Letitia's apartment building. 'So what do we do?'

'I thought you could wear a mask.'

'He'll recognise my hair.'

'Pin it up and get a wig, a black wig.'

'It might work.'

'If I don't do it I think he'll go elsewhere. Then I won't be able to help Matthew.'

Ursula leant over and put her hand on Letitia's knee. 'Are you doing anything tonight?'

Letitia shook her head. Ursula grinned. 'Then I think if we're going to give Piers a performance, we should go inside and start to rehearse.

The Rolls-Royce pulled up outside the Mayfair house. The driver got out and opened the rear door for his two passengers. He led the way to the front door and opened it for them.

It had all been arranged. Letitia had explained to Piers that she had been thinking about his suggestion and had remembered a girl at her last job who'd made a very obvious pass at her at the firm's Christmas party. When Letitia had phoned her and asked her if she would be willing, the woman had jumped at the chance and had no objection to Piers' presence provided he could not see her face. She wanted to wear a mask. Fortunately Piers appeared to find that suggestion exciting. It added to the theatricality and he liked that.

Ursula was already wearing a brunette wig, its tight curls falling to her shoulders. As soon as the chauffeur had left, she took a stiff black velvet mask from her handbag. She had bought it in a theatrical costumier's yesterday. It covered her eyes and was moulded to the contours of her cheeks and the bridge of her nose, the material edged in a frilly white satin and encrusted with glitter.

The housekeeper had been given the night off. The

house was quiet. Piers had promised he would not take a peek as they got out of the car. He was sitting in a back bedroom, waiting until the clock struck eight thirty. Only then was he allowed out. So far Letitia was sure he'd kept his word. She checked all the windows carefully.

'Come on,' she said, leading the way up to the master bedroom.

'Beautiful paintings,' Ursula said, admiring the oils that hung on the wall all the way up the staircase. 'Is that a Van Dyck?'

'I've just had a thought, do you think he'll recognise your voice?'

'Possibly. I'll keep the conversation to a minimum.'

'Good. Come on then.'

Letitia felt her heart beginning to thump against her chest as she opened the bedroom door. Three days earlier, in her tiny bedroom, she had gone to bed with Ursula for a second time. It had been better than before, she thought, not only because she had known what to expect but because this time she had also been more confident and was totally in control. Of course the addition of the vibrator had something to do with it too. The thought of repeating the performance in front of Piers filled her with a peculiar, almost sickly-sweet anticipation.

'So what do we do now?' Ursula said, keeping her voice low in case Piers was within earshot. She glanced around the bedroom before sitting on the big double bed. As usual the counterpane had been stripped back to reveal the white linen sheets and matching pillowcases, crisp and uncreased. But there was no lingerie neatly laid out on it. Piers clearly thought that the presence of two women was excitement enough.

Letitia came to sit beside her. 'There's something

exciting about it being so clinical and matter-of-fact, isn't there?' Ursula was wearing a button-fronted emerald-green silk dress with a deep V-neck. Letitia put her hand on her knee and slid it up under the hem, where she felt the glossy champagne-coloured nylon Ursula was wearing giving way to soft flesh. She turned and kissed Ursula on the lips as her hand dug down between her thighs, feeling the silk of the panties that covered her sex. She plunged her tongue into her mouth and Ursula sucked it gently, then pushed forward with her own, the two dancing together, hot and wet.

'God, I'm getting turned on,' Ursula whispered. 'You really want it, don't you?'

'I'm getting greedy, I suppose,' Letitia said, standing up. It was true. Greedy and demanding. Her new-found sexual awareness had made her more assertive and intrepid and that in itself was exhilarating. She was wearing a white blouse and grey slacks. She began to unbutton the blouse.

'When is Piers going to turn up?'

Letitia stripped off the blouse. She was wearing a sample of her own design, a black jacquard three-quarter-cup underwired bra with a clasp at the front, the cups angled slightly to give greater lift and definition. 'Let's not worry about him.'

She shucked herself out of the slacks. Her panties were her own design too, a string bikini, the elongated triangle of the sleek material at the front tapering off into a string on the hips with a similar triangle stretched tightly over the bottom. She was wearing BSL black stockings too, the hold-up variety, their wide elasticated tops dimpling the flesh of her thighs.

Ursula was looking at her admiringly.

'Don't you think you're a little overdressed?' Letitia said. She caught hold of Ursula's hands, pulled her to

163

her feet and began unbuttoning the dress. She slipped it off over her shoulders and let it fall to the floor. Ursula was wearing a white satin bra, a matching white suspender belt, its long narrow suspenders clipped into the champagne-coloured stockings, and thong-cut panties that revealed the creases of her pelvis.

'I thought it was tarty enough,' Ursula said.

'I'm a little surprised he hasn't left anything he wants us to wear.'

Letitia went to the bedside chest. Its top drawer was already open. She looked inside. There was no scarf this time, just the vibrator and the bottle of perfume.

'We do have to wear this,' she said, picking up the perfume. She took the stopper out of the bottle and dabbed it against Ursula's throat, and between her breasts and thighs.

'I think I remember Sharon used this,' Ursula said, sniffing the air.

Letitia applied the perfume to her own body, then put the bottle down. Kicking off her shoes, she lay on the bed. She closed her eyes for a moment to allow herself to concentrate on the feelings of excitement that were swirling through her. In the last two weeks she had lain here six or seven times waiting for Piers, her body usually swathed in silk or lace, often tight and constricting, knowing exactly what he expected of her, waiting to perform what many might consider a weird ritual. The fact that it was so premeditated, so cold and calculating, made it different from any sex she'd ever had, but, she knew, that was also what made it so exciting.

She felt Ursula's hand stroking her thigh. It moved over the top of her stocking and up to her mons, caressing the material of her panties. Immediately Letitia's clitoris pulsed, eager to draw attention to itself.

She felt Ursula's fingers gripping the thin waistband and lifted her hips to allow her to draw the panties down her long legs.

'Now that's a pretty sight,' Ursula murmured.

Letitia opened her eyes. Ursula was gazing at the apex of her thighs, her neat, stubbly pubic hair hiding little. She knelt up on the bed and dipped her head down to Letitia's belly, kissing the soft flat flesh. Her mouth moved over to Letitia's hip, then traced its way down the crease of her pelvis until it reached her pubes.

The fact that it was a woman doing this to her, and not a man, was still new enough to add piquancy to everything Letitia felt, the thrill of the forbidden never far away. She spread her legs further apart, stretching them across the bed.

'Is that a hint?' Ursula said teasingly.

She ran her hand down Letitia's thigh, allowing the side of her little finger to graze her labia. They were hot and sticky. Very slowly she moved her hand back up again, this time pressing a little more deeply so her little finger slid into the fleshy gap. Then, quite suddenly, she swivelled around on her knees, so her bottom was pointing at Letitia's face and her legs were at her side, and dipped her head down between Letitia's thighs, locking her mouth to her sex, and kissing it hard, crushing her lips against Letitia's labia. The tip of her tongue darted out and began to circle Letitia's clit, producing an immediate wave of pleasure.

Letitia moaned. She raised her head to look at Ursula. Bent forward like this, her bottom thrust into the air, her neat labia were pursed between her buttocks tightly covered in the white silk of her panties. Letitia caressed her bottom, smoothing her palm against the soft flesh. She prodded her fingers under the gusset of the panties and down between Ursula's thighs until she could feel her labia. They were as hot and wet as her own. She pushed her middle finger up until she found Ursula's swollen clit and began to circle it, at the same speed Ursula was using on her.

Their bodies undulated gently, swaying to the cadence of the waves of pleasure that washed over them. There was no urgency at the moment, just wonderfully tender sensuality.

'Lovely,' Letitia breathed.

'Mmm . . .' Ursula agreed without moving her mouth.

Letitia reached out with her left hand to the open drawer of the bedside chest. She managed to rummage around inside until her fingers wrapped around the shaft of the vibrator. She slid her right hand from Ursula's sex and used it to pull the narrow gusset of the panties well over to one side. Then she nosed the vibrator into Ursula's labia, the thin, hairless lips throbbing visibly as they were pushed aside.

Letitia heard Ursula gasp as the cold plastic shaft butted into her vagina. She could see the way her labia folded around it, almost as if welcoming it with a kiss. She pushed it deeper. There was no resistance; Ursula's sex was quite as liquid as her own. In one smooth motion the vibrator all but disappeared, only the gnarled knob at the butt end visible. Letitia felt Ursula's reaction to this penetration, a gasp of pleasure creating an exhaust of hot air that played over her own sex, Ursula's tongue temporarily distracted. But it was only temporary. As soon as the initial wave of pleasure abated it went back to work, circling the little nut of nerves with delicacy and precision.

Letitia sat up slightly so she could reach the gnarled control switch, then twisted it on. The humming noise was muted but Letitia thought she could actually see

Ursula's labia, stretched tightly around the broad phallus, begin to vibrate.

This time Ursula's reaction was more violent. She reared her head up from Letitia's sex and cried out loud. Her hands, which had worked their way under Letitia's thighs, clutched at the flesh, her fingers digging into it like claws.

'So good . . .' she managed to gasp. She thrust back on the dildo, pushing it deeper. 'Right there, right there,' she said, rotating her hips.

With her free hand Letitia lifted Ursula's left leg and swung it up and over her body, so Ursula was straddling her chest. She squirmed down the bed until Ursula's sex was right over her mouth then, still holding the dildo firmly in her vagina, reached up and managed to thrust her tongue between the tops of Ursula's labia and on to her clit.

Ursula's whole body shuddered at this sudden intrusion. Letitia could actually see her labia clutching tightly around the base of the phallus as she felt her clit spasming wildly against her tongue. The older woman's body went rigid, she threw her head back once again and a long low-pitched cry escaped from her mouth. Then, just as suddenly, she seemed to melt, all resistance thawing away, her body slack and sluggish.

'That was so quick,' she muttered as the orgasm melted away.

Letitia rested her head back on the bed, allowing the dildo to slither out of Ursula's vagina, then turning it off. She bent her legs at the knee and flexed her belly upward. It was her turn now.

Ursula took the hint. 'Give me the vibrator,' she said.

As Letitia placed it in her hand, its shaft still glistening with viscous sap, Ursula dipped her head again and began to lap at the blonde's sex. This time she licked the whole length of it, her tongue buried deep in the slit. The inner surface of Letitia's labia was so sensitive, she thought she could feel the tiny papillae of Ursula's tongue grating against it. The fact was that Ursula's orgasm had set all Letitia's nerves on edge. She had not only been able to see her coming, she had felt it too, the empathy between them total.

As Ursula's tongue sawed to and fro, provoking intense waves of the most wonderful sensations, Letitia heard a very slight noise. She looked over to the bedroom door and saw Piers padding in, the silk paisley robe wrapped around his slender frame. He came over to the bed and sat in his wing chair. He didn't smile or acknowledge her in any way. His face was set in a serious, almost grim, expression.

The thought of him there created an even stronger wave of feeling, as she had known it would. It felt depraved to let a man watch her like this, being so lewdly handled by another woman, but as with all the depraved and bizarre sexual scenarios she had worked her way through in the last few weeks, that was also profoundly exciting. She had this odd feeling of seeing herself from above, seeing her body stretched out on the bed with Ursula poised above it and Piers sitting in the chair observing every action. Her clitoris throbbed.

Ursula must have seen Piers too, because she dropped her voice an octave when she sat up and said, 'Turn over.' The black mask made it difficult to read her expression, though Letitia thought she detected a new glint of excitement in her eyes.

She was certainly determined to play to her new audience. She reached behind her back and unclipped her bra, though looking at Letitia, not at him. Her heavy breasts quivered as they tumbled out of the white satin and she shook her shoulders from side to side, making them slap against each other forcefully. Then she seized her nipples and pulled her breasts outwards by them, until they formed pyramids, the pulpy flesh striated by being so stretched.

Allowing her breasts to drop, the flesh slapping against her ribs, she raised herself and pulled her panties down to her knees, then rocked back on her bottom and tugged them off her legs. She very slowly and very deliberately scissored her legs apart and stroked the neat, hairless plain of her sex. Dipping a finger into her vagina with equal wantonness she pushed it deep then withdrew it and sucked it into her mouth, this time looking directly at Piers. Letitia thought the bulge that distended the front of his robe twitched visibly.

'Get on your hands and knees on top of me,' Ursula said, still trying to disguise her voice.

As Ursula lay on her back Letitia got up on all fours on top of her, arranging herself so that her legs straddled Ursula's head and her hands were planted on either side of her hips, with her buttocks pointing at Piers.

Ursula reached up, unclipped Letitia's front-opening bra, and pulled it away. Briefly she kneaded Letitia's breasts, pressing the pliant flesh back against her ribs. She tweaked both her nipples, using her fingernails to bite more effectively, then wriggled down the bed until she could reach them with her mouth. She sucked the left nipple hard, then tweaked it with her teeth before flicking it from side to side with the tip of her tongue. Moving to the right, she repeated the process.

Letitia gasped. Her breasts had never felt so sensitive. Her nipples were on fire.

Scrambling back up the bed, Ursula hooked her arms around Letitia's back and levered herself up until she could get her tongue on the little crater of her anus, slathering it with her saliva.

Letitia was intensely conscious of Piers' eyes, as if they were emitting rays of heat that burnt into her. It made her buttocks prickle as she felt Ursula's hands caressing them. The first touch of the plastic dildo made her start. Ursula slipped it between her labia and forced it hard against her clit before turning it on, the humming noise not as muffled now.

'Oh God,' Letitia moaned. A huge surge of sensation rolled over her, making her whole body clench. But Ursula immediately moved the dildo away, sliding it along her labia. She played it briefly around the mouth of her vagina, then settled the tip into the little round hole of her anus.

'Yes.' The word was almost imperceptible. It came from Piers. Letitia dropped her head and looked down her body and between her legs. She could glimpse Piers, leaning forward, his eyes locked on her rump, a look of total lust making his face seem almost gaunt.

Ursula pressed the tip of the vibrator into Letitia's anus. As she felt her sphincter give way, and the smooth plastic slid inside, she remembered how Andrew had felt as he'd buggered her. She had never had an experience like that. Her vagina contracted sharply as the dildo inched deeper, Ursula's saliva lubricating its passage.

'No,' Letitia breathed. It was the same pain she had felt before and her reaction to it was the same. She desperately wanted it to stop, but at the same time frantically hoped and prayed it would go on forever. It was pain at exactly the same frequency as pleasure and soon it was impossible to distinguish between the two.

The dildo stopped, buried deeply inside her most private passage. The vibrations spread out like ripples on a pond, making the silky tube of her vagina vibrate first, then, seemingly, the whole of her belly. Ursula's finger was on the move again, slipping up the slit of her sex to her hard, swollen clitoris. It began to nudge it from side to side.

Letitia was coming. Her whole body was locked around the broad plastic phallus. But even in the midst of the waves of pleasure that crashed through her senses she was aware of Piers. She wanted to see him watching her. That was the extra dimension, the old fantasy, adding piquancy to everything she felt. With an effort of will she fought the desire to close her eyes and took one last look down her body, her breasts hanging like teardrops, her thighs banded by the black stocking tops, to where Piers was sitting. She could see he had hardly moved, his eyes still riveted on her body, his hand rubbing against the front of the robe.

And then her orgasm overwhelmed her. She cried out loud, as Ursula's finger unerringly found the most sensitive spot on her clit, sending sparks flying out into her body like electric shocks. Her anus and vagina went into spasm and she screwed her eyes closed, allowing the sharp, violent feelings to wash everything else away.

Chapter Seven

'*COME IN, PLEASE.*'

'Thank you.'

Letitia was wearing her best business suit. It was black, with a short jacket and a knee-length skirt.

'Do sit down.'

Gordon Prentiss' office was surprisingly small. It was square and crowded, bookshelves on every wall crammed full of box files. He had a small Victorian partner's desk with an inlaid leather top, which was also so loaded down with files and paper that only the old-fashioned leather blotter immediately facing him was free. Even the computer keyboard and monitor on one side and a telephone console on the other were beginning to disappear under the chaos of paper.

Letitia sat in a small, modern, straight-backed chair, one of two in front of the desk.

'I'm sorry to make you come in on Saturday,' he said. 'It's just that after my trip I had a lot to catch up on and I can work better here than at home.'

'It's better for me actually,' Letitia said.

'Good. Look, I hope I haven't got you here under false pretences. I was very impressed with your attitude at that do but I don't think we've got any call for more lingerie.'

'I only wanted to show you my stuff.'

'Have you got samples?'

'Yes.' Letitia was carrying a voluminous nylon holdall, the samples all carefully wrapped in tissue paper.

Gordon cleared the telephone console of files and punched a button on it. A squeaky voice rang out from the speaker.

'Yes, Mr Prentiss.'

'Are the girls still here?'

'I think so.'

'Good. Ask them to stay for a few minutes, would you? I want them to do a bit of modelling.'

'Certainly, sir.'

Gordon turned back to Letitia. 'We're finishing off a photo-shoot downstairs this morning,' he explained. 'Better to let the girls model the stuff than me seeing it over the top of my desk.'

'Absolutely,' Letitia said enthusiastically.

'There's ten of them. I'm sure two or three will be the right fit.' He hit the button on the telephone console again. 'Marcia, would you take Ms Drew down to the studio.'

Thirty minutes later Letitia had organised the girls to model the range of lingerie she had brought, two girls wearing the basques, two in the slips, bras and panties, and another in the matching suspender belts. They were all experienced on the catwalk and would do quick changes behind the scenes to illustrate the three different colourways the samples had been made up in. As the top-selling brassière size was a 36B and the panties a size ten, lingerie samples were all made in that size, and eight of the ten fitted them exactly.

The photo-shoot had been for a new range of swimwear, so a set had been built with a beach complete with deckchairs, loungers, a picnic hamper, sand, a sandcastle and a background of blue sky. It was not ideal for slinky lingerie but it was a great deal better than Prentiss' office.

Marcia, Gordon's secretary, a jolly but rather dumpy brunette had helped Letitia with all the arrangements, then called her boss to tell them they were ready. She stole three of the deckchairs from the set and set them up in front of the area where the girls would parade.

'All ready?' Gordon said as he stepped through the studio doors. He was holding a mug of coffee in his hand.

'As ready as we'll ever be,' Letitia said, feeling suddenly nervous. She was sure, from what he had said upstairs, that this was probably a waste of time, but she couldn't help feeling anxious.

Gordon sat in the middle deckchair, with Marcia to his right, her notepad at the ready. 'OK,' he said.

The girls were lined up behind the huge backdrop of blue sky. Letitia signalled that the first should come forward.

Very professionally, swinging her hips from side to side in the exaggerated way that most models adopted, the girl walked across the 'beach'. She was wearing a thigh-length black slip, made from the new stretchy, silky material that BSL had developed. The slip hugged her body. Had she had any bulges in the wrong places, which she did not, it would have smoothed them away. The bodice, however, was made from a fine, almost transparent, lace.

The next girl wore the half slip in the same material and Letitia's new three-quarter-cup bra in a deep hunter green. The bra lifted her breasts and held them together, creating a deep cleavage.

And so it went on. Letitia left what she considered

the best until last. Joy had wanted her to create an unconventional basque and she had done just that. The new material BSL had developed could also be made in an almost transparent version, like the finest chiffon but with a glossy feel and as clinging and stretchy and supportive as Lycra. Letitia had used this to create a basque with long suspenders extending out from the apex of four triangles jutting out from the hem. The top of the bodice, the bra straps and the hem were finished with satin ribbon. The way it clung to and shaped the body, veiling but not concealing it, and with no boning, seemed almost miraculous. She had designed little panties in the same material.

After the first parade the girls changed and demonstrated the other colours. The pellucid basque came in cappuccino, a gun-metal grey and a light pink, the satin ribboning a matching but deeper colour, the pink lined in a deep rose red. It was the colours that Letitia was most proud of, the new material making them alluring and lustrous.

'That's it,' Letitia said, as the girl in the pink basque walked behind the blue backdrop.

Gordon Prentiss said nothing for a moment. He sipped his coffee, which must have been stone cold, then turned to Marcia. 'Is the photographer still here?'

'I think so.'

'See if you can find him. Ask the girls to stay on for another hour. I'd like some snaps of these things. Nothing too professional. Just so I can show them to Bebe.'

Marcia got to her feet, smiled an encouraging smile at Letitia, then walked out through the studio door.

'I'm very impressed.' Gordon said quietly. 'It's just right for us. A lot of lingerie has gone over the top, too much into the bedroom and not enough practicality.

This does both. It's stuff women could wear during the day and still look great in if they suddenly find themselves in a strange bedroom.' He laughed. He had a lovely open laugh like the tinkling of a piano. 'If you know what I mean.'

'That's what I had in mind,' she said.

'Good. Look, I've got a lot to get through today. I know this sounds like an imposition but I don't suppose you're free for dinner tonight? I'd really like to discuss this with you.'

'I'd like that too.'

'Good. Eight o'clock. I'll come and pick you up. Give Marcia the address. What sort of food do you like?'

'Anything.'

'That could be dangerous. What about Italian?'

'Fine by me.'

She was getting used to chauffeur driven cars. Gordon Prentiss' was not a Rolls-Royce, however, but a huge, rather square Mercedes with a voluminous interior, deep pile carpets and all the equipment she'd first seen in Piers' car. And like the Silver Wraith a glass partition separated the driver from the passenger compartment.

'Would like you another drink?' Gordon said, indicating the walnut- veneered cocktail cabinet.

'No, I've had quite enough. What was that stuff?'

'The dessert wine? Vin Santo. People think it's communion wine, but it's not.'

'It was delicious.'

'I'm glad you enjoyed it.'

'I enjoyed the whole meal.'

Gordon had taken her to a small and intimate Italian restaurant where the food had been sensational. They had had pasta with salami, ricotta cheese and rocket, followed by a seafood platter that had been almost like

176

a stew, with lobster, mussels, clams, red mullet, prawns and monkfish all cooked together. A sensational zabaglione had been served as dessert with the Vin Santo and little almond biscuits that Gordon had told her could be dunked in the wine.

They had talked business for most of the evening. He had asked her all about the availability of materials and colours, the size range, and the length of production runs, all of which, she was delighted to say, she had boned up on, with Daniel Travis and Joy Skinner's help, before she came out. His attention to detail and his range of knowledge had surprised her. He was not, after all, the lingerie buyer for his group, but the chairman and chief executive.

She was also surprised that she found it hard to take her eyes off him, especially when he talked. He had a way of moving his rather thick, fleshy lips that fascinated her, and he wore a strong aftershave that she liked. She liked his eyes too. Even in the midst of a discussion on how many thong-cut panties they would need to order to set up a production run, they seemed to have a soft, self-deprecating expression that undercut his professional business manner.

'So we've talked about your designs,' Gordon said, as the Mercedes skirted the north side of Regent's Park. 'What about you? How did you get into all this?'

'I always wanted to be a designer. I did a textile design course but got a couple of dead-end jobs. Then, when I started at BSL I began thinking about lingerie. It's funny, I'd never really considered it before. I used to be a cotton-knickers-from-M-and-S girl.'

'And now?' He raised an eyebrow.

'Now I get free samples. But, I mean, it can be very erotic, don't you think?'

'It's like all the best presents come gift-wrapped.'

'Exactly. What about you? How did you get started?'

'I ran a stall in a market. Then two stalls. It all grew from there. I just seemed to have a knack for knowing what people wanted to wear.'

'Some knack.'

'Look, this is a bit awkward . . .'

'Go on.'

'I have to run all this by Bebe Kay, my lingerie buyer. I love the stuff but I can't ignore her.'

'Of course not.'

'It'll take three or four days before we can come up with something positive, you understand that?'

'Of course.'

'It's just that . . .' The confidence and assurance he had showed all evening had melted away. 'I don't want you to think I'm trying to . . . I mean . . . I'm hopeless at this.' He took a deep breath. 'I just wondered if I might see you again. Nothing to do with business this time. Oh, I haven't asked you if you're in a relationship. I can see you're not married . . .' He nodded towards her left hand.

'I'm not.' She certainly didn't count Piers as being 'in a relationship'.

'I just would hate you to think I'm using business as a lever to get you to go out with me. If you don't want to see me again it won't affect our business dealings, I can promise you that.' He looked absolutely sincere, his face set in an expression that begged her to accept that he meant what he said.

'I don't.'

'You don't want to see me again?' He looked grief-stricken.

'No. I don't think you're using business as a lever, and I'd love to see you again, Gordon. I really would.'

His face reminded her of a puppy dog that had just been given its favourite toy. 'That's great.'

178

The Mercedes had just passed through Camden and was heading towards Kentish Town. In a minute or two they would be outside her front door.

'Can I ask you something now?'

'Of course.'

'According to my copy of *Cosmopolitan*, a lot of men don't like it if women make the running. Is that true?'

'I have no idea,' he said, looking puzzled.

'Is it true in your case?'

'I don't think so.'

'Can you be any more definite?'

'I don't see it makes any difference.'

'Where do you live?' she asked.

'Hampstead.'

'Would you take me there?'

'Of course.'

'Now. Would you take me there now, Gordon? I think you're a very attractive man. I understand about the business side of things. This is nothing to do with that. I just don't want the evening to end. I don't want to end up in bed on my own, thinking about you, when I could end up in your bed with you. Does that make sense? If it puts you off, you'd better say so.' As little as five weeks ago Letitia would never have dreamt of being so forthright. But whatever else the last weeks had taught her, she had learnt that she had nothing to lose by expressing her feelings. In the past she would have pussy-footed her way around the idea that she found Gordon attractive and wanted to go to bed with him. Now she knew exactly what she wanted and had the confidence to go about getting it.

Without a moment's hesitation, Gordon Prentiss pressed a small button on the console set in the panelling above the side armrest. The glass partition whirred down.

179

'Bill, change of plan. We're going home.'

'Certainly, sir,' the chauffeur replied.

The car slowed, and took the first left-hand turn as the glass partition whirred back up again.

'That was decisive,' Letitia said.

'I didn't want you to think I was put off.' He turned towards her, his eyes looking into hers for a second as if trying to read some hidden message, then leant forward, cupping her cheeks in his hands, and kissing her on the mouth, his tongue thrusting between her lips, his body pushing her back against the leather seat.

She felt a rush of desire. She wrapped her arms around him and kissed him back hard, crushing their lips together and sucking on his tongue. His body felt hard and powerful. She managed to insinuate her hand under his jacket and caress his back through his shirt.

'I've wanted to do that all evening,' he said, his lips still so close to hers she could feel them move as he spoke.

'Me too,' she said breathlessly. She pushed forward, catching his bottom lip between her teeth and nibbling on it, then kissing his cheeks and his chin hungrily, before settling on his mouth again, her tongue pushing forward this time. Her mouth was hot and wet and, inevitably it seemed, so was her sex, the connection between the two established instantaneously.

He moved his mouth to her cheeks, her nose and her ears, kissing and sucking at her flesh as she threw her head back. She was wearing her black cocktail dress with the V-neckline and he kissed her throat, tonguing the hollow at the top of her collarbone.

'God, I want you,' he whispered.

'Can you feel my heart beating? I'm so turned on.'

His hands were all over her, sliding up and down her dress, over her legs, around her breasts. She could see the

180

chauffeur's eyes in the rearview mirror focused on her left leg, where Gordon's hand had rucked up her skirt to expose the top of the glossy black stockings she was wearing. Though it had been turned into a living reality in the last few weeks, her fantasy, the idea of being watched, was still potent. In another mood Letitia might have spread her legs apart and encouraged Gordon to explore her nether regions more intimately, allowing the chauffeur to see a great deal more. But tonight Gordon was providing her with more than enough excitement and she modestly pulled her skirt down over her thigh. The chauffeur's eyes switched back to the road.

The car was climbing Rosslyn Hill now, with Hampstead Heath on the right-hand side. It turned left into one of the narrow tree-lined streets and came to a halt in front of tall wrought-iron gates set into a red-brick wall. The gates were opened by electric motors and the Mercedes swept into a gravel drive in front of a large Victorian house.

'Looks like we're here,' Letitia said, sitting up. She glanced into Gordon's lap. His navy-blue trousers were tented by a bulging erection.

The chauffeur opened the passenger door and Letitia climbed out. There was a gleam in his eye which she pointedly ignored.

'Thanks, Bill,' Gordon said as he got out too. 'See you on Monday at eight.'

'Goodnight, sir,' Bill said, with no expression. He got back into the car and drove it out through the gates.

Gordon took out his front door keys.

'Have you got servants?' Letitia asked.

'Cook and a housekeeper. But they don't live in. I hate that. No privacy.'

He opened the front door and ushered her inside. He slammed it closed with his foot as he gathered her in his arms again, kissing her full on the mouth, his head bent down to reach. As his tongue invaded her mouth, he wrapped one arm under her knees and lifted her off her feet with as little effort as if she had been a feather pillow. Still kissing her, he walked down the hall and up the long straight staircase.

Letitia's heart was racing. She kissed him back hard, her hand at the back of his neck, pressing him closer, her tongue dancing against his. She was hardly aware of the inside of the house, her lust taking all her attention.

The door of the master bedroom was ajar. Gordon leant against it with his back, then carried her inside. He walked over to the double bed and laid her on it, folding himself down on top of her, the kiss still unbroken. She felt his hand running up her leg again, pushing the skirt of the dress up. It moved over the top of her leg and down between her thighs. In one seamless movement two of his fingers had nudged aside the gusset of the black silk panties she was wearing, found the opening of her vagina and pushed right up inside until his knuckles were hard up against her labia.

Letitia gasped. If she had been wearing tights, this easy and instant access would not have been possible. Stockings had that distinct advantage. It felt as if he was scissoring his fingers apart, stretching the velvety flesh inside her sex. At the same time his tongue seemed to push deeper into her mouth. She was momentarily swamped by a wave of pleasure. Trying to wrestle herself back under control, she pushed her hand down between their bellies and found his erection, squeezing it hard. She ran her hand up to the waistband of his trousers, undid his belt and the top of his fly, pulled down his zip, then fished inside. His cock had pushed its way out of the fly of his boxer shorts and she felt the hot flesh respond as she closed her fingers around it.

She rubbed the ring of her finger and thumb over the distinct ridge at the base of his glans and he moaned, the sound forced out into her mouth.

His fingers left her body and she felt them dragging her panties down her legs. She lifted her bottom off the bed. As he was so much taller than she was, he managed to pull them down to her knee without the need to break the kiss. She, as eager as he was not to interrupt the wonderful sensations their mouths were generating, immediately drew up her left leg and extracted it from the leg of the panties, leaving the black silk hanging from her right.

Instantly he tore her hand away from his cock and rolled on top of her as she spread her legs apart. He pulled his head back so he was looking down at her, his eyes glinting with passion as he bucked his hips, and his cock rode up into her on a tide of her juices, filling her, completing her.

She cried out loud, feeling her sex closing around him, his erection as hard as steel.

'That's what I wanted,' he said.

He kissed her again. The double impact of his hot tongue and his hot penis penetrating her at the same time produced a wave of feeling that threatened to overwhelm her again. His cock was big and reached deep into her vagina, stretching it in every direction. That matched her whole response to him; it was so instant, so basic, a purely animal thing, it had buried itself in her psyche as deeply as he was buried in her sex.

But she fought it. She wanted to give as good as she got and wrapped her arms around his back so she could lever her belly up against him, meeting each forward thrust with a thrust of her own. Her hands grabbed the waistband of his trousers and pulled them down over his bottom. As soon as they were banded around his thighs she moved her hands up again, caressing the firm, muscled flesh. She pushed a finger down into the cleft between his buttocks, found the puckered flesh of his anus, and wriggled her finger inside.

He gasped, rearing his head up off her. He stopped hammering into her and raised himself on straight arms, his body bent like a long bow, his cock thrust so deeply into her its base was crushed against her clitoris. He stayed like that for what seemed like an eternity, his eyes staring down at her, an expression of wild lust locked into every feature of his face. Then he dropped down on to her again, his chest crushing her breasts, his phallus ploughing in and out of her, every muscle in his body seemingly concentrated on that one movement.

Letitia's body reacted instantly. The combination of the hard, hot sword of flesh thrusting so forcibly into her vagina and the hammering it was giving her clitoris was irresistible. She was hot, with her clothes still tangled around her body, and sweat was beading her forehead. But the fact that his desire for her was so great he simply hadn't been able to wait even the few seconds it would have taken to pull her dress off was exciting. Everything was exciting. She felt her orgasm beginning to build, her sex clutching convulsively at his cock, each spasm bringing her closer to the inevitable. She had had a lot of sex in the last few weeks but this was completely different; this was sex at an instinctive level, without forethought or calculation, without anything but the phallus that pulsed inside her.

Gordon thrust forward again and this time she had the sensation that her sex was opening for him, like a flower, the petals folding back to allow him in. There, right at the top of her vagina, he invaded a secret place where a whole new set of nerves, raw and unused,

184

responded with feelings that literally took her breath away.

'Oh God, God, God . . .' She contrived to push her finger a little deeper into his anus. But that was all she could do. Her body heaved, every nerve singing a symphony of pleasure as they reached a climax together, her whole world focused on her sex and the whirling feelings it generated. But just as she thought that the feelings could get no more profound, at that exact moment his cock bucked up into her one last time and began to jerk violently against the tight tube of her vagina. She felt the hot, viscous fluid of his semen spattering into that secret place, and instantly it triggered a whole new set of sensations, taking her body to another level, higher-pitched, deeper-felt, more intense. She cried out loud, a longer mewling noise, her head thrust back against the pillow, her mouth wide open, her mind unable to register anything but the sensation of pleasure.

He was naked. He stood in the bathroom doorway with two long glass flutes in one hand and a bottle of Dom Perignon in the other.

'Champagne,' he said. 'It seemed appropriate.'

'Mmm . . . I'd love a glass.' Letitia was sitting in a big white bath in his blue-tiled bathroom.

Gordon put the glasses down on the bath surround and opened the bottle with a pop. He managed to catch the overflowing wine in one of the glasses.

'You look very sexy like that,' he said.

'Like what?'

'Up to your tits in bubbles.'

Letitia had added bubble bath to the water, and her breasts were floating on the surface, surrounded by white foam.

He handed her a glass. 'Here's to spontaneity,' he said, sitting on the side of the bath.

'I'll definitely drink to that.'

They clinked glasses. The champagne was delicious. Letitia put the glass down again and lay back in the water. Her body was still tingling, the nerve endings in her vagina and her clitoris delivering little pangs of protest at the rough treatment they had received. Some were more noticeable than others, some of the large trills taking her breath away, but all were apparently determined to make sure Letitia could not forget for one second what had just happened to her.

'I love those black stockings,' he said.

'Black stockings are what started all this.'

'What does that mean?'

'I never used to wear stockings. When I went to my interview at BSL they gave me a pair. They seemed to have interesting side effects.' She thought she wouldn't mention Matthew Silverstone's influence.

'Really? Like what?'

'Let's leave it at that for the moment. I don't want to tell you all my secrets tonight or you'll get bored and never want to see me again.'

'I want to see you again.'

'That's because you want to know all my secrets.'

'Are there a lot?'

'Yes. No, not really. I'm very ordinary, Gordon.'

'Rubbish. You're a great designer. Pity you haven't got some of your samples here. I might demand another look with you as the model this time.'

'I'll have to do something else to keep your interest then.'

'What have you got in mind?'

She knew exactly what she wanted. And what was even better was that she knew exactly how to get it. All her inhibitions had gone. That was one thing she would always be grateful to Matthew Silverstone for. He'd started her off on this road after all.

'Stand up.' Looking at Gordon's naked body, Letitia felt a strong surge of desire. With his clothes on he looked as if he were thin and rather weedy, whereas in fact his muscles were strong and well defined. Oddly, despite the thick growth of hair on his head, he had very little body hair, his skin smooth and tanned.

Gordon got to his feet.

'Closer,' Letitia ordered. She knelt in the middle of the bath with her elbows resting on its side.

Before he could move closer, Letitia raised her hand and grasped his cock, water and soap suds dripping on the tiled floor. It was still completely flaccid, his circumcised glans smooth and pink. She pulled him by it until he was standing right at the edge of the bath. Then she fed his cock into her mouth. He moaned loudly.

Instantly, as she ran her tongue over the soft flesh, she felt her sex throb, aware of a soreness that added to the piquancy of the pleasure. She opened her lips wider and reeled in his scrotum too, until both his balls were in her mouth. She could taste her own juices.

Gordon reached down and cupped her left breast in his hand. 'I'm sorry these were badly neglected before,' he said, squeezing the malleable flesh. The nipples were still erect and he pinched them gently between his fingers.

She felt his penis stir. It had only been twenty minutes since he had come so explosively but it began to swell rapidly. Letitia tongued his balls, jiggling them up and down, but as his phallus engorged it pushed into her throat and she was unable to contain them any longer. As his balls spilled out from her lips one by one, she cupped them in her right hand.

187

In seconds he was fully erect. She sucked him deep right into her throat, then pulled back, working her tongue against the ridge at the base of his glans. His cock pulsed. While she squeezed his scrotum gently in her hand she pulled her mouth off his now rigid phallus and worked her lips all the way down the outer surface, where the bulging tube of the urethra distended his flesh. She nibbled and sucked at this right down to the base of the shaft and back up again. Then she pulled his cock down and worked her lips along the underside until they were grazing his pubic hair. Again she travelled back up to the glans, this time plunging her mouth down on him, letting him relish its heat and wetness.

Gordon would only take so much of this treatment. He seized her by the shoulders and pulled her to her feet.

'Let me,' she said, sulkily.

'No. I want you. Get out of the bath.'

It was her turn to obey. As she stepped out of the bath, water streaming from her body, he bent his legs at the knee, moved his arms around the top of her thighs and hoisted her smoothly off her feet, until her belly was at the same level as his. She saw what he wanted to do immediately and wrapped her legs around his back and her arms around his neck, her sex poised above his erection.

Slowly he lowered her on to him. The water had washed away the natural lubrication from her labia and they were dry. However hard he pressed his phallus into the mouth of her vagina it made no progress. But suddenly, like a seal breaking, her labia parted and he was thrusting up inside her, the interior as wet and warm and welcoming as it had been earlier.

'Oh God, Gordon, you feel so good,' she said, her mouth pressed to his ear.

His hands were underneath her thighs, supporting her weight. He lowered her further, his cock plunging deeper, until it was completely buried in her and she could feel the base of it hard against her clit.

She wriggled from side to side, grinding her clitoris against him, and felt her sex clench tightly around his cock. It wasn't going to take much to make her come again.

He lifted her, pulling her off him until only his glans was still inside her, then dropped her down on to him again, her whole weight thrusting him back so forcibly it took her breath away. He lifted her again, holding her off longer this time. She moaned in anticipation just before he dropped her again, his steel-hard phallus lancing into her. She was coming. There was something about this position, her sex suspended in mid-air, her labia pursed around the rigid rod of his erection, that was intensely exciting. She buried her face in his neck, thrust her pubis forward against his to crush her clit between their two bodies, then came, a sharp, intense orgasm that reached into the feelings she had had before and renewed them.

As the passion drained away, he pulled out of her and put her down, turning her around so she was facing the bath. She got the idea immediately. Grasping the top of the bath she leant over and thrust her bottom out at him. 'Is this what you want?'

He answered by plunging his cock into the cleft of her buttocks. She felt its heat nosing into her labia. There was no dryness now. She had the impression her vagina had winked open, eager to suck him in. He thrust up into it powerfully, his hands holding her hips. But after two or three strokes he slowed and pulled out, moving his now soaking-wet glans to the puckered crater of her anus.

'You have to tell me if it's all right,' he said.

Letitia moved her hand back between her legs. She caught hold of his phallus, then held it steady as she pushed herself back on it. She felt her sphincter resist. She pushed hard and it gave way, and suddenly he was inside the hot, tight sheath of her anus. As she pushed back again it slid deeper, the juices from her sex that had smeared his cock lubricating its passage. The familiar mélange of feelings flooded over her, the pain and the peculiar and vicious pleasure it produced.

Gordon began to thrust of his own accord, gently at first but then with increasing power. Each thrust produced a whole gamut of sensations in Letitia, from pain to ecstasy and back again, except it was not that simple, because the pain was striated with pleasure and the pleasure with pain. All Letitia knew was that she was coming again. She started to shout, each inward thrust he made producing a throaty 'Oh!' The tempo of the thrusts got quicker and the noise she was making louder. Finally he stopped, pulling her back on him one last time. She felt his cock swell, then kick, and as his semen spattered out into her, she came too, her whole body rigid.

Eventually, after what seemed like a long, long time, the rigidity melted away and she felt as if she were floating, drifting lazily in a glorious tide of sticky pleasure.

Chapter Eight

'WHAT DID HE SAY?'

'He's going to let me know this week. He has to check it all out with his lingerie buyer.'

'Bebe?' Joy Skinner looked depressed.

'Yes. What's the matter?'

'She's a first-class cow. She's on the take. She wants a big kickback before she gives anyone an order. That's why she's stuck with Mirage all this time.'

'Really?'

'Really.'

'Can't Gordon override her?'

'He never has before.'

'It might be different this time.'

Joy sat back in her chair. Though she had been given a large office on the first floor she still preferred to do most of her work in the studio, in the thick of everything that was going on, though she had imported a new desk and a computer terminal. 'Don't get too optimistic. It doesn't matter anyway. It's still a great line and it's going in the catalogue. That's not bad for someone who's only been working here six weeks.'

'No. I suppose not. Anyway, I thought I should tell you what was going on.'

'Let me know as soon as you hear.'

'I will.'

Letitia wandered back up to her office. It was Monday morning and the euphoria of the weekend had begun to fade. She had spent the night at Gordon Prentiss' house, and found him indefatigable, waking as the early-morning sun leaked through the curtains to find him pressing his body into her back, his mouth sucking at her neck and his erection nestling into her buttocks. They had made love again and again, until they were both simply exhausted.

He'd asked her to stay for lunch but she'd declined, deciding things were moving too fast and she needed some time alone.

The rest of Sunday seemed to have passed in a haze, every muscle in her body in a sort of numbed state, her nipples and sex positively sore from overuse. Her mind was numbed too, unable to really focus on what had happened, still trying to digest it.

During the course of the day, as she thought about it all, she became more and more depressed. She supposed that Gordon could have his pick of a number of women. He was unmarried and rich, and even if he was not as attractive as Matthew Silverstone, he was certainly personable. What had happened with her undoubtedly happened on a regular basis with other women; his sexual prowess was evidence of that. As far as she was concerned, what had happened was very special indeed, sexually as well as emotionally. She realised that the whole time she had been with him she hadn't once thought about Ursula or Matthew or even Piers Green. He had wiped the slate clean. But unfortunately she couldn't convince herself he would think of their night together as anything out of the ordinary.

At least that was what she told herself. She didn't want to make a fool of herself by reading more into their evening together than there actually was. She was sure Gordon liked her and was certain he found her attractive, but he probably felt exactly the same about a dozen women he had seen in the last two or three months.

That conviction grew when he didn't call her on Sunday afternoon or Sunday night. It was set in concrete when he didn't call her on Monday morning. And by Monday afternoon she was telling herself she had better try and forget him. She had been a fling, another conquest to notch up on his belt, his avowed protestations that he was eager to see her again the usual hollow insincerities.

But for all her conviction her nerves still jangled every time the phone rang.

At five it rang for about the eleventh time.

'Letitia Drew,' she said, trying to stop her heart beating so fast.

'Letitia, it's Ursula.'

Ursula was the last person she wanted to hear from.

'Hello,' she said weakly.

'I wondered if you'd had a chance to talk to Piers.'

'Piers? No. About what?'

'I thought we'd agreed. About Matthew. You said if I co-operated . . .'

'Oh yes, right. I'm sorry, I'm in the middle of something,'

'You did say you'd try, Letitia. I think I've kept my side of the bargain.'

'I know, and I will.'

'Why don't we go to the Bruniswick tonight? Take a room. We could have room service. I feel like some company.'

'No,' Letitia said quickly. 'I've got to meet a friend.'

'Come on, Letitia,' Ursula said seductively. 'I need you.'

'I can't.'

'All right. But do speak to him, honey. It's important. Tell him he can have a return engagement any time he wants. It would be fun, wouldn't it?'

'Yes,' she said, though she wasn't at all convinced.

'Are you sure you don't want to let me pick you up? It would just be you and me and room service. Who knows what we could get up to?'

'No, Ursula, I can't,' Letitia said decisively.

'Another time then.' Ursula's voice was suddenly cold.

'I'll call you.'

'Don't leave it too long.'

Almost before Letitia had put the receiver back on its cradle it had rung again.

'Hello, Letitia Drew.'

'Sweetie, it's Piers.'

'Oh,' She couldn't raise herself to sound enthusiastic. After the straightforward passion of Saturday night, the complicated games Piers wanted to play seemed remote and uninspiring.

'You sound down in the dumps.'

'No, just had a busy day.' She tried to sound more chipper, reminding herself that Piers still offered a lot of advantages. If she wasn't going to have Gordon, she supposed she could raise herself to perform for Piers. In fact, she decided, in order to cheer herself up, an expensive dinner might well be just what the doctor ordered. 'I hope you're ringing me up to ask me out to dinner,' she said coquettishly.

'You read my mind. Shall I pick you up?'

'Please. Just give me time to get home and have a bath.'

'About seven thirty?'

'Perfect. Thank you, Piers.'

'My pleasure, my dear.'

She smiled. She would make sure it *was* his pleasure. But as much as she tried to pretend it was what she wanted to do, she couldn't stop wishing it was Gordon Prentiss' Mercedes, not Piers' Rolls-Royce, that was coming to pick her up.

'You look quite lovely tonight.'

'Thank you, Piers.'

She was wearing a strapless tube dress in a turquoise blue, its stretchy material clinging to her body. Her own design of strapless bra supported her breasts, pushing them into a generous cleavage which the dress flattered perfectly.

'I wish you'd let me get you a little something . . .'

They had been through this before. Piers had offered to set up accounts for her at the leading Bond Street couture houses, but Letitia had refused. She didn't want to feel like she was his official mistress, bought and paid for.

'I like to make my own way, Piers, you know that. I don't want your gifts.

He smiled. 'I understand,' he said.

Letitia wasn't sure she did. She loved clothes. It would be a delight to trawl through St Laurent, Prada and Gucci and be able to buy whatever she wanted. But she couldn't let herself do it. She was already indebted to Piers for her promotion.

'But there is something you could do for me.'

'What's that?'

'The Silverstones.'

They had eaten a lobster mousse wrapped in spinach and a grilled sea bass with *beurre blanc*. Letitia had refused dessert but had made inroads into a plate of *petits fours* that had come with the espresso coffee. La

Poulette was crowded, the restaurant glittering with candlelight, each pink-linen-covered table provided with a slender white candle in a silver holder. They had the best table, in a corner, with a view of the floodlit gardens at the back.

'What about them?' She had expected the name to produce some sort of response, but he maintained his equanimity.

'I think I may have misinterpreted what happened.'

'Misinterpreted?'

'I think Ursula . . . I was probably more responsible than I like to admit to myself. It was the first time I had done anything like that, and perhaps I was afraid to admit that I really liked it.'

'It appears that you do.'

'You saw that for yourself,' she said. 'I'm more comfortable with it now.'

'So what do you want me to do?'

'I don't know. I just thought it wasn't fair on Matthew if . . .'

He put his hand on top of hers to stop her, a moment of rare physical contact.

'I always intended to have Joy Skinner take over BSL,' he said. 'It was time for Matthew to move on.'

'I understood he was in line to take over another company.'

'He was.'

'Past tense.'

'No. I haven't made up my mind yet. He needs to prove himself to me.'

'And how can he do that?'

'My dear, if you are worried that Matthew won't get what's coming to him because of the way he treated you, then don't be. I would have hoped that he would have behaved better but I'm not a hypocrite. After what we've done over the last two weeks I can hardly berate him for sexual peccadilloes, now can I?'

'No.'

'Good.'

A waiter arrived to ask if they wanted more coffee. They both refused, but Piers asked for the bill.

'You know, Letitia, what you've done . . . don't think I don't appreciate it.'

'I know you do.'

'After my wife died, I thought . . . I didn't think I'd ever find a woman who would understand. I thought of going to prostitutes, but that's not very dignified, is it?'

'No.'

'I have something rather special in mind for tonight.'

'Oh.' She tried to smile. Despite her conviction that Gordon Prentiss was definitely not going to ring her, she had been thoroughly disappointed when there were no messages on her answerphone when she got home. She was still thinking about him. She had thought about him all evening. She wanted to feel herself being literally swept off her feet again. She wanted that hard, large erection buried inside her. But she had accepted Piers' hospitality and certainly wasn't going to cry off now.

'It's a little surprise,' he said.

'I like surprises,' Letitia told him, though she wasn't sure it was true.

The shiny claret-coloured Rolls-Royce Silver Wraith glided up to the restaurant entrance as the *maître d'* escorted them to the door with heartfelt hopes that they had enjoyed their meal and would return again. His attention was not surprising considering the price of the wines Piers had ordered.

Inside the car Piers stretched out, putting his head back against the leather head restraint and closing his eyes.

'That was a beautiful meal,' Letitia said.

'It was, wasn't it? Do you know, Letitia, just being with you makes me feel excited. Perhaps exhilarated would be a better word.'

'That's because you're thinking about what I'm going to do.'

'Yes. It is.'

Letitia began to think about it too. For the first time since she had left Gordon she felt a twinge of desire. Her body was still sore but she knew it would not take long to get herself aroused. She would stretch herself across Piers' bed and use the plastic vibrator while she remembered everything Gordon had done to her on Saturday night and Sunday morning. If she couldn't have the real thing, at least she had learnt to find a substitute.

The car delivered them to Piers' front door. The house was in darkness apart from a light on the first-floor landing.

'Housekeeper off again?' Letitia asked.

'Definitely.' Piers let them in and turned on the lights.

'What about the alarm?' Letitia asked. She remembered he had turned it off the last time they had been in the house alone.

'It's all right,' he said vaguely. 'Would you like another drink?'

'A brandy.'

They walked through into the sitting room and he poured two brandies into big balloon glasses, then handed her one, sitting down next to her on a large leather chesterfield.

'So what have you got planned?' she asked. She found, a little to her surprise, that the first signs of arousal were already pricking at her nerves.

'Why don't you get more comfortable? May I?' Piers leant forward and touched the front of her dress. He hooked his fingers in the bodice and pulled it down, revealing Letitia's strapless cream bra. It was the first time he'd ever made any attempt to undress her. He was staring at her breasts.

'Why don't you undo my bra too?' she said, only momentarily taken aback. Turning around, she offered him the catch and felt his fingers fumbling with it. Suddenly it was free and the bra fell away. Her breasts quivered.

'And now my dress.' She stood right in front of him. He pulled the tight material over her hips and down her long legs. She was wearing stockings and a cream suspender belt but no panties. She had dressed that way to excite herself as much as him, and it worked. She felt a strong surge of arousal as she saw his eyes staring at her short pubic hair. For a moment she thought he was going to lean forward and kiss her belly, but he didn't.

'Lovely,' he breathed.

'What is this, Piers? You've never wanted to do this before.'

'Trust me, my dear. This is rather special.' He got to his feet. 'I wanted to see you down here. I wanted to see you walk upstairs.'

'Interesting . . . I can see you've been plotting something.'

'Shall we go?'

He took her hand, touching it as though it were extremely fragile and might break, and led her back into the hall. She climbed the stairs ahead of him, intensely aware of his eyes burning into her buttocks. She wondered if he would be able to see her labia. He certainly had a good view of the white suspender belt and the tan-coloured stockings, the welts pulled into taut peaks on her thighs.

'Are we going to the bedroom?' she asked on the landing.

'Yes. But first . . .' He fumbled in his jacket pocket and pulled out a black silk sleeping mask. 'I want you to wear this.' He unfurled the mask and stretched it out between his fingers. 'They say that when one sense is removed, all the others become increasingly sensitive, especially the sense of touch.'

Letitia wasn't sure how to react. This was all entirely new for Piers, way outside anything he'd asked her to do before. But there was something titillating about standing here naked apart from her suspender belt, stockings and a pair of black court shoes, while Piers was still fully dressed.

'All right,' she said.

'Turn around.'

She turned her back on him and he lifted the black silk over her head and rested it down over her eyes. It was padded on the inside and shaped around the bridge of the nose so very little light got through. She had pinned her hair up into a French pleat and Piers carefully fitted the elasticated straps of the mask over it and around her ears.

'Now what?' she said. In the almost total darkness the first thing she was aware of was the beat of her heart. She started slightly when she felt his hand on her arm. She heard the bedroom door creak open. She had never been aware that it creaked before.

It was true that all her senses seemed to have been cranked up by the loss of her sight. Immediately she stepped forward she smelt the scent of the perfume that was kept in the bedside chest, Sharon's perfume. It was stronger than it had ever been.

Piers' hand guided her forward, then halted her in her tracks.

'Wait here,' he whispered in her ear.

'What do you want me to do?' she asked.

'Just wait.'

She heard his footsteps moving away. A light clicked on, so loudly it sounded like a rifle shot. He had gone into the bathroom. The door closed behind him. Letitia stood and waited. The blindfold seemed to have increased the awareness of her own body too. She could feel her nipples stiffening by the moment, and her sex had moistened to such an extent that her labia were wet and slippery. The next noise startled her. It sounded like someone getting off the bed.

'Don't worry, it's only me.'

The voice belonged to Ursula.

'Christ, what are you doing here?' Letitia was about to raise her hand and tear the blindfold off, but Ursula caught her by the wrist.

'Don't spoil it for him.'

'What are you doing here?'

'I called him this afternoon.'

'You called him?'

'Don't worry. I told him I was the lady in the black mask. I suggested this little scenario. He was only too willing. Don't tell me you're not excited. I can see it for myself.' She flattened the palm of her hand against Letitia's left breast, grinding the nipple back into the surrounding flesh.

Letitia's shock had turned to a rush of arousal. She abandoned herself to it. She didn't like the idea of Ursula talking to Piers direct and manipulating him to get her own way, but she didn't want to think about all that now. Her sexual urges were too strong. This afternoon the idea of making love with Ursula again hadn't been in the least appealing, but now her body appeared to have other ideas. She wanted to wipe away the memory of Gordon Prentiss. That was what she was here for, after all, and when it came down to it Ursula could help her do that far more effectively than she could have done it on her own with Piers. Ursula's hand moved up to her face. She stroked her cheek then kissed her on the mouth. Letitia wrapped her arms around the other woman's back and pulled her closer, flattening her body against hers, and kissing her hard, plunging her tongue into her mouth. She was wearing something silky, a basque, Letitia thought, in satin. She ran her hand down over her buttocks and felt the long finger of a suspender at the side of her thigh and the shiny nylon of her stockings. Ursula had dressed for the part.

'Over here,' Ursula said, breaking the kiss. She took Letitia's hand and moved her to the bed, turning her around until she felt the mattress against the back of her knees. 'Sit.'

Letitia sat down. She felt Ursula sit beside her, then push her back on the bed. The undersheet felt warm, where Ursula had been lying, no doubt.

'Why the blindfold?'

'It's exciting, isn't it?'

A hand was moving up her leg, caressing the silky nylon of the stocking. It got to her thigh, then gently pulled her leg to one side. Letitia co-operated, imagining Ursula staring into her open sex. None of this was what she'd been expecting tonight, but it was enormously stimulating.

She heard the bathroom door opening. Footsteps padded across the floor. The springs of the wing chair creaked slightly as Piers sat down in it. Letitia opened her legs wider.

'Lovely,' Piers said softly. 'So lovely.'

Letitia felt movement on the bed. The cool satin of Ursula's basque settled at her side. Ursula's hand cupped her right breast, squeezing it softly. Then Letitia felt her mouth closing over the nipple. She sucked it hard, then pinched it with her teeth. Leaning over Letitia's body, she applied the same treatment to the other breast.

The blindfold had made Letitia passive. She lay back enjoying the sensations Ursula was giving her without feeling the need to reciprocate. This was all Ursula's idea after all. If she wanted her so badly, she could take her.

She felt Ursula's hand running down over her navel. As her mouth went back to her left breast, sucking her nipple in and this time flicking it gently with her tongue, her hand moulded itself to the curve of Letitia's pubis, her palm over her mons, her middle finger slotting into her labia. Immediately Letitia felt the sharp pang of feeling as Ursula found her clit.

'She's so sensitive,' Piers said.

'Yes, she is,' Ursula agreed.

This was new. Piers had never shown any desire to communicate, sitting in his chair without comment before.

The finger nudged Letitia's clitoris from side to side. She felt it pulse. She could imagine Piers sitting in the chair in his silk paisley robe, watching her, his hand in his lap.

'Together,' she said, without making any attempt to move.

'And I thought you didn't want me,' Ursula said mockingly.

Her weight moved on the mattress. Letitia felt her thigh swinging over her shoulders. The scent of the perfume wafted over her face.

'Is that what you wanted?'

For the first time Letitia moved of her own accord.

She reached up and hooked her hands around Ursula's thighs, then levered her head up. Her mouth butted against Ursula's buttocks. She angled it lowered until she could feel the soft folds of her sex, just as Ursula dipped her head and planted her mouth on Letitia's sex. And there it was again, that unforgettable feeling of being joined, like they had become one. It sent shivers through her body, as though she had been plugged into some incredible source of sexual energy. Everything she felt was doubled. Ursula's hot, wet tongue was flattening itself against her clit, at exactly the same moment, she found Ursula's bulbous, swollen clitoris with her own.

Waves of the most intense pleasure swept through her, just as she felt them sweeping through Ursula. The bra of the basque was pressing against her tummy and she could feel the older woman's heavy breasts trembling. Hers, unencumbered, were squashed against the satin that covered Ursula's navel. With all this provocation it was only a matter of seconds before the powerful sensations that were coursing through her body amalgamated into one single, throbbing whole that was propelling her rapidly towards orgasm.

She felt Ursula's hand working its way under her buttocks, and the tips of her fingers wriggling into her labia. She raised her own hand to do the same, working it over Ursula's buttocks, feeling her way downward until the soft, wet flesh of her sex was butting against her fingertips. She thrust two fingers into Ursula's vagina. The feeling of it, tight and wet and incredibly silky, sent a shudder of pleasure through her body, just as Ursula's fingers plunged into her own vagina.

She knew Ursula was coming too. She could feel it almost as acutely as she could feel herself. Her vagina was rippling and her clitoris pulsing, in exactly the same way as Letitia's were. Their bodies were undulating against each other, each prone to sudden peaks of pleasure that seized their nerves as if they had been struck by lightning. Desperately, trying to ignore her own feelings, Letitia tongued Ursula's clit and twisted her fingers deeper into her sex. And Ursula did the same to her. They had become one. And, at one and the same time, their movements stopped, their mouths pressed against each other's sex, a stifled cry escaping their lips, their orgasms crashing over them in concert, their bodies suddenly rigid.

It felt as though it went on for hours. Like a storm trapped in a deep valley, Letitia's orgasm rattled around her body, unwilling to let her free, finding new areas of sensitivity to provoke. Finally Ursula pulled herself up and moved away.

But Ursula had not finished with her. Letitia felt her hands on her hips pushing her on to her stomach. In a wonderful fog of insensibility she allowed herself to be rolled over. She felt hands caressing her buttocks and the backs of her thighs and spread her legs apart again, not minding if they explored in more intimate places. She was by no means sated; as had become usual in this new life she led, her first orgasm had only created a desire for more.

But the hands didn't move inward. Instead they travelled down her legs, caressing the glossy nylon.

There was a movement behind her on the bed, a weight settling between her legs. The hands on her hips were picking her up, pulling her bottom into the air. Again she co-operated, allowing herself to be brought up on to all floors, the fog still enveloping all her senses.

She felt both Ursula's hands going to work on her breasts, lightly pinching her nipples, and producing little trills of pleasure. But the fog was beginning to clear. If Ursula's hands were at her breasts, who was holding her hips? Piers? Could it be Piers?

The hands pulled her back strongly. Her bottom butted against a hard, hot cock.

'Oh God,' she said, wriggling against it. 'That's wonderful.'

It was. It was exactly what she needed. After the soft, delicate touch of a woman, what better than a hard, strong, thrusting man?

Ursula was kneeling at her side, the satin basque brushing against her body. She felt her hand skating down over her back. She must have seized the cock because she felt it jerk against her buttocks. Ursula was guiding it down between Letitia's legs. It slid into her labia and up into her vagina.

'Does that feel good?' It was Piers asking this question.

'She's so wet,' a man's voice said.

'Just hold it there. I've never seen this before. I like to see it like that.'

That was the second shock. The voice was not Piers'. It belonged to another man. Letitia recognised it too but could not place it. She didn't care. She didn't care about anything apart from getting that rock-hard phallus deep inside her. Her clitoris was throbbing wildly, this new surprise only increasing her excitement. If the man, whoever he was, didn't push forward soon, she thought she would come like this.

'I think you should give her what she wants now,' Piers said. He was directing this performance.

Immediately she felt Ursula's hand move away and the big hard cock thrust forward. The silky flesh of Letitia's vagina parted as it rode up into her, filling her completely. It was only then, only as the glans rapped against the neck of her womb, that she realised whose the voice was. It was Matthew Silverstone's.

A hand was snaking down the front of her belly. It delved into her labia and found her clit, working it from side to side. Letitia was already coming and this new stimulus only accelerated it. Was it Matthew's hand or Ursula's? Who was still squeezing her breast? Was the fact that she didn't know increasing her excitement? She screamed as her orgasm exploded, provoked by her mind quite as much as by her body, the thrill of the forbidden, of knowing this was all completely debauched and depraved, almost as strong as the knowledge that Piers was watching them all, his eyes noting every detail.

Matthew's cock began jerking inside her, spattering hot semen into the depths of her body, his excitement obviously as extreme as hers. But she was too exhausted to respond, the demands of her own orgasm having taken everything out of her this time.

Thick, viscous liquid seeped down the velvety walls of her vagina. But as they both came down from their mutual high, as Matthew's cock softened and slipped out of her and she collapsed back on to her stomach again, something happened. It was as though she had been doused in cold water. There was no glowing aftermath of orgasm, and no desire for more. She felt only a growing numbness.

She rolled over and sat up, pulling off the blindfold.

Matthew was kissing his wife, their arms wrapped around each other. Ursula was not wearing her mask and Letitia realised she had not been disguising her voice. Piers was sitting in his wing chair, a damp stain spreading over the front of his robe. Ursula broke the kiss and burrowed down on to the bed to suck her husband's flaccid cock into her mouth. He moaned loudly.

'You taste so good,' she said, momentarily breaking away and staring up at Letitia.

'I want to see you with Matthew this time,' Piers said, still clearly in the mood for more.

Letitia got up. She climbed into her shoes and walked to the bedroom door.

'Where are you going, my dear?' Piers asked without looking away from the bed. 'You'll get your turn again, don't worry.'

She did not answer. She walked downstairs and found her clothes.

She put them on as quickly as she could, then let herself out of the front door. She found herself on the street. The air felt hot and humid. There were people walking by and traffic on the road. She began to walk towards the main road. Then she began to run. She wanted to get away from that house and everything it represented as fast as she possibly could.

It was a good photograph. Matthew Silverstone sat behind a large rosewood desk. Over his shoulder, through a floor-to-ceiling window, was a view of Canary Wharf. Matthew was trying to look serious, as befitted a photograph for the financial sections, but there was a smile, even a smug smile, lurking beneath the unruffled exterior.

Letitia read the story under the photograph again. Matthew Silverstone, it had been announced yesterday, was to take over Greystone Retail, a large retail group which was part of Green Gross Friar Holdings. He was to be succeeded at BSL by Joy Skinner. There was a long interview with him detailing his aims for the company, which, according to him, had been underperforming.

After what had happened last night it was not a surprise. Ursula had lied to her. She had decided that she was not going to get what she wanted from Letitia and had gone direct to Piers. At what point she had revealed her identity to him Letitia didn't know, but she had obviously judged it just right. She had promised him all sorts of delights and last night had delivered the first instalment. Clearly, if Piers had thought he would be embarrassed by Ursula's presence, he had quickly changed his mind. Having taken the first few halting steps with Letitia, he was now prepared to be more daring, not only with his choice of subjects but in what he wanted to see. He could hardly take a moral stance for the way the Silverstones had treated Letitia now that he had allowed them to see his own sexual peccadilloes. Through his wife's persistence, Matthew Silverstone had got his company.

In fact, Letitia felt no resentment, nor regret. She had gone into everything she had done with Piers with her eyes open. She had been excited and exhilarated by it. But last night her journey of exploration had gone too far. And she knew why. Gordon Prentiss. If she had not met him she doubted she would have reacted the way she had. Sex with Gordon had been gloriously uncomplicated though no less intense, and that was precisely what she realised she wanted and needed now. Nothing more or less. The irony of it was that having at last found a man who could give her exactly that and wasn't married, he appeared totally uninterested in her.

Finishing her morning coffee, Letitia grabbed her handbag and her keys and was just about to head out of the front door when the phone rang.

The name of Gordon Prentiss flashed up in her mind in bright-blue neon. She ran to the phone.

'Hello.'

'Letitia?' It was Piers Green.

'Yes,' she said, with no emotion.

'How are you? Did you get home all right?'

209

'Yes thank you.'

'Why did you leave in such a hurry?' The line was indistinct and kept fading. She was sure he was phoning from his car.

'I think you know that, Piers.'

'You seemed to be having such a good time.'

'I was. I mean . . .' If he didn't understand it she wasn't sure how she could explain it to him. 'I think I made a mistake.'

'A mistake?'

'Look, Piers, if that's what you want that's fine. But it's not for me. Not any more. I tried. I experimented. But I don't want to do it again.' This wasn't coming out right, but she couldn't think what to say.

'That makes me sound like some sort of pervert,' he said sharply.

'No, that's not what I meant.'

'I thought you were enjoying yourself. I thought you were having a good time.'

'I was.'

'It doesn't sound like it. It sounds like you were doing it for altogether other reasons. What was it, Letitia? Were you trying to make sure you got the right job at BSL? Is that it?'

'No. No, of course not. I'd just had enough. I need something else.'

'I want you to come around tomorrow night.'

'Is Ursula going to be there?'

'She's had a rather amusing idea. It'll be fun.'

'No, Piers.'

'What did you say?'

'No. I'm not coming.'

'I want you there, Letitia,' he said, his voice so flat and uncompromising she hardly recognised it.

'No. I don't want that any more.'

'Is that your last word?'

'Yes.'

'I think you should consider your position most carefully, don't you? BSL is my company, Letitia.'

'What does that mean?'

'Exactly what I say. I suggest you think things over very carefully.' The friendly, solicitous manner had disappeared. This was a different Piers, the man used to getting his own way.

The dialling tone erupted in her ear. Piers had clearly slammed the phone down. She hadn't handled that well at all, she thought. It looked as though she had jumped from the frying pan into the fire. Ursula had made her leap through a number of sexual hoops in order to keep her job and it appeared Piers was now determined to do the same thing.

Outside the weather had turned and the hot sunshine had given way to cloud and occasional showers. It had the advantage of making the tube less stuffy. She arrived at BSL just after nine.

'Joy Skinner wants to see you,' the receptionist said the moment she walked through the door.

'Where is she?'

'In Matthew's office.'

'Right.'

'There's someone with her.'

'Really?' Letitia had no need to ask who. She allowed herself an ironic smile. It hadn't taken Piers long to deliver on his threat. She walked up the stairs to the first floor. Jackie was sitting at her desk outside Matthew's office.

'Hi,' she said cheerily. 'You can go right in.'

Letitia knocked on the door and opened it without waiting for a reply.

'You want to see me?'

Joy was wearing a voluminous black tunic top over baggy black trousers. She was seated at her desk, while Piers Green stood behind her staring out of the window. Three or four boxes of files were stacked on Matthew's old desk

'Good morning,' Piers said, turning around. As usual he was immaculately dressed, his Savile Row tailored grey suit fitting him like a glove. He wore a crisp white shirt and a dark-red tie.

'What is it?' she said, in no mood to be toyed with.

Piers nodded to Joy. They had obviously rehearsed what was going to be said.

'Bad news, I'm afraid, Letitia,' she said, her eyes only meeting Letitia's for a second.

'Oh?'

'We've had a change of heart on the new lines. We're going to pull your range from the next catalogue.'

'Really? I wonder why?' she said, staring at Piers.

Joy looked distinctly uncomfortable. 'These things happen. Look, perhaps it would be better if you came back to the studio for a while.'

'I'm being demoted too?'

'Not really. It would be good for you to work with the others again.'

'I thought you liked my stuff. I thought Daniel was mad about them.'

Letitia had the impression that Joy was just about to say something else, then changed her mind. 'Let's just leave it at that, shall we?'

Piers was watching her expression beadily.

'Fine,' Letitia said. Piers Green had made his point. He had obviously called Joy the moment he had put the phone down on Letitia and diverted his car to BSL's offices to meet his new managing director. 'Is there anything else?'

'I'm sorry, Letitia.'

'Don't be.' At least Joy had the decency to look embarrassed.

'Of course,' Piers said, 'this need not be permanent. It's all a question of working together as a team. Of co-operation. If you show a little more co-operation then I'm sure BSL will be happy to reassess your work. Isn't that right, Joy?'

Joy did not reply.

'I know exactly the sort of co-operation you want, Piers.' Letitia turned to Joy. 'I'm leaving, Joy. I should have done this right at the beginning. It's my own fault. I was playing with fire and I guess I just got burnt. I should never have got involved.'

'There's no need for that,' Piers snapped. 'Be reasonable.'

'There's every need. I should have done it weeks ago.'

'If it was up to me . . .' Joy started to say.

'I know, I'm not blaming you,' Letitia said quietly, actually feeling sorry for the woman. Without another word she walked out of the office and closed the door.

Back in her own small office, she sat behind her desk and stared into space. She felt stunned, but she had known from the tone of Piers' voice this morning that he was not going to take rejection lying down. The truth was exactly what she had told Joy. She had played with fire. She should never have got involved with Matthew Silverstone knowing he was a married man. Everything else had followed from that.

Of course she could have rung Piers and told him she'd changed her mind. She had another option too. She was sure the tabloid press would be happy to hear that Piers Green's devotion to moral rearmament was only skin deep. They might even pay her for her story.

But she was sure that no one in the fashion business would ever take her seriously again if she appeared on the front page of the *Sun* no doubt decked out, on their insistence, in an outfit with considerable décolletage. She preferred to go quietly and rebuild her career with another firm. She still had all her designs after all. Perhaps Mirage would be interested

The knock on the door startled her.

'Come in.'

'Hi.' Gordon Prentiss stood in the doorway grinning from ear to ear. He was carrying a slim pigskin brief-case.

'Gordon!' She jumped to her feet. She was so astonished to see him she stood with her mouth wide open.

'I hope you didn't mind me turning up here.' He came up to her and kissed her on both cheeks. He was wearing the musky aftershave that she remembered from Saturday night.

'Of course not,' she managed to say.

'I wanted to see you. I missed you. Does that sound crazy?'

'No. Why didn't you call me yesterday?'

'I didn't want to call you until I had some news. Then this morning, after I talked to Bebe, I thought I'd come and see you in person. Besides, I wanted to sort out my feelings.'

'Feelings?' Letitia had so thoroughly convinced herself that Saturday night had been no more than a one-night stand for him that this astonished her too.

'Yes. Look, tell me if I'm making a fool of myself but I thought what happened between us was really special.'

'It was for me too, but I thought . . .'

'What?' He looked genuinely puzzled.

'I thought that I was just one in a long line.'

He laughed. 'I'm not saying there haven't been others, but that's what I mean. There was something between us, something I hadn't felt before. I really want to see you again, Letitia. Could we have dinner tonight, or is that too soon?'

'That would be lovely.'

'Great. Look, you know I told you that we weren't going to mix business and pleasure, that I'd have to let Bebe decide about the lingerie?'

'Yes.' Here it comes, she thought. He was going to tell her that Bebe didn't like her designs and was going to stick with Mirage.

'Well, Bebe thinks they're sensational. But there's more. We've been negotiating to buy a chain of lingerie and accessory stores in the States. It's my first venture over there. If that goes through Bebe thinks we can lead with your range. I've got all the numbers, if you want to go through them.' He patted his briefcase.

'That's great news,' Her mind was spinning. 'I think we'd better go and talk to Joy.' She picked up the phone, deciding that this wasn't the moment to tell Gordon her news. She hoped Piers was still there.

Five minutes later she was standing in Matthew Silverstone's old office again, with Gordon at her side. Piers was sitting on the red chesterfield.

'So you want the whole range?' Joy said, from behind her desk.

'Yes. Bebe has worked out the colourways and the size variations based on our customer profile, but obviously once we get the American end on board that will change. We're talking at least fifty thousand units to begin with and an option on a further one hundred thousand for England. For America we'll start with two hundred thousand with an option on three. Presumably you can handle that volume?'

'We can,' Joy said coolly, looking at Letitia.

'This is very good news,' Piers added.

'Of course we would want Letitia to supervise the whole order from start to finish. We also want to commission her to work on a new line exclusively for us. Presumably that won't be a problem?'

'Gordon, there's something I haven't told you,' Letitia said.

'What's that?'

'I no longer work for BSL.'

'What!'

'Letitia, my dear, I thought that was settled. You seem to have got hold of the wrong end of the stick.'

'If Miss Drew doesn't work here any more I don't think we'd feel confident in placing such a big order,' Gordon said at once.

'My dear boy,' Piers continued, 'there's no problem. Letitia misunderstood what we were trying to tell her a little earlier, that's all.'

Letitia smiled sweetly. 'Oh, I see,' she said. 'So my designs are going into the catalogue as planned?'

'Absolutely,' Piers said.

'And of course you must keep your office. We've been experimenting with new working arrangements, Gordon, but we all think Letitia works better in her own environment,' Joy added, smiling broadly. Having been forced to demote Letitia, she was now delighted Piers was getting some of his own medicine.

'I see.' Gordon was looking puzzled. He turned to Letitia. 'Is there a problem then?' he asked.

'Apparently not. I'd be happy to oversee everything.'

'Well, if that's the case I'd better get Bebe in here this afternoon to go over everything with you. There is still the little matter of price.'

'We'll be happy to meet with her,' Joy said.

216

'Good. So that all seems to be settled.'

'Indeed,' Piers said. He got to his feet. 'I hope there are no hard feelings, Letitia. Perhaps we could have dinner tonight to discuss your future?'

'Sorry,' Gordon said at once, 'She's having dinner with me.'

'More champagne?'

'No.'

'More anything?'

'Oh yes.' Letitia got to her feet. She was naked apart from a pair of BSL's silky, incredibly glossy black hold-up stockings. She cleared away the remains of the smoked salmon, caviar and king-sized prawns they had been picnicking off in the middle of Gordon's large bed. She laid the food on the floor then scrambled across the bed. 'There's a lot more I want.'

'Like what, for instance?'

'Like this.' She knelt beside Gordon's naked body. He had picked her up from work at six and they'd driven straight to his house. They had been in bed ever since, pausing only to raid the refrigerator and bring food and champagne up to the bedroom. She gathered his flaccid cock in her hand. She had discovered that the ridge at the bottom of his glans was incredibly sensitive and began rubbing it with her thumb. He moaned.

'That's my weak spot,' he said. His cock began to swell in her hand. She watched it, fascinated by how rapidly it engorged. 'Now look what you've done.'

'I'm sure we can find a use for it.'

She dipped her head down and sucked his erection deep into her mouth. At the same time she swung her leg over his chest so she was straddling his body, then pushed herself backward until her sex was poised above his mouth. Her clitoris began to throb. It had already taken a terrible pounding as he'd made love to her in a variety of positions, but the tenderness only increased its sensitivity.

Gordon reached up and licked the whole slit of her sex. He lapped at her juices, his tongue so hot it made her vagina pulse.

'Lovely,' she said, the word half muffled on his phallus. He had ejaculated in every orifice of her body bar one, and now she was going to make up for that omission. She tongued the ridge of his glans then began working her mouth up and down on him, her hand snaking down between his thighs to gather up his scrotum and squeeze it gently in her hand.

'You'll make me come,' he breathed before going back to her sex, his tongue winkling out her clitoris.

'That's what I want,' she said

And it was. The wonderful thing was that despite all the bizarre and extraordinarily exciting experiences she had had, she knew this was precisely what she wanted most. She felt his cock pulsing in her mouth and knew, what was more, that it was precisely what he wanted too.